Acknowledgments

I want to thank everyone involved in Pitch-a-Palooza. There was some question as to whether or not this idea could be extended into book length, and I myself wasn't sure either. But you guys voted for it and inspired me to try like a motherfucker to make it work. It was difficult at times, but I'm happy with the result. I hope you are as well.

Toilet Baby

Shane McKenzie

ERASERHEAD PRESS
PORTLAND, OREGON

ERASERHEAD PRESS
PO BOX 10065
PORTLAND, OR 97296

WWW.ERASERHEADPRESS.COM

ISBN: 978-1-62105-153-4

Printed in the USA.

This book is dedicated to all the attendees of Bizarrocon 2012 who witnessed the first toilet baby's conception. She's doing well, and getting big!

Chapter One

Grady sprinkled sawdust on the puddle of vomit. He breathed through his mouth so he wouldn't have to smell it, though all that did was baste his tongue in the essence of it. He could handle the smell of shit and spoiled food and all other manner of offensive odors, but if enough vomit stink swirled into his nostrils, he was sure to add to the pile himself.

And I can't do that...she's watching me.

The sick little boy who had emptied his belly onto the classroom floor had had spaghetti last night, and it didn't look like he was a very thorough chewer. The sawdust turned the bile into brown mud, but did nothing to conceal the coiled-up pile of noodles.

After Grady scooped up the mess and tossed it into the garbage bag on his cart, he wiped the coat of sweat from his forehead with his sleeve and faced the teacher, Ms. Flowers, who had gone on with her English lesson as Grady worked. Some of the other kids snickered at him, which he had grown used to. He didn't hold it against them. Poop and other gross things were funny to kids, and as the janitor, he supposed he was the Master of Gross.

Ms. Flowers was calling on the kids one at a time so they could read a passage from *Where the Red Fern Grows.* As a little girl began reading, the teacher—the most gorgeous woman Grady had ever seen—shot him a quick look, and the tiniest smile hooked the corner of her mouth.

"All done here, Ms. Flowers," Grady said, louder than he meant to.

The little girl stopped mid-sentence, and with the rest of the class, spun her head to stare at Grady as he smiled stupidly at the teacher.

"Thank you, Grady," Ms. Flowers said, then sort of

curled her lips over her teeth and shot her eyebrows up her forehead.

"S-sorry," Grady said with a wave, then wheeled his cart toward the door and out into the hallway. The kids chuckled a bit behind him before getting back to their book.

The Master of Gross just made a jackass out of himself, boys and girls.

This was the most he'd ever said to the lovely Ms. Flowers, never really knew how to approach her before. He always hoped she would have some kind of mess for him to clean up so he could get close to her, but he guessed a pile of noodley puke wasn't the best of ice breakers.

A woman like that would have no interest in the janitor, Grady. In your dreams, buddy.

He gave the classroom door a long look before finally shambling up the hallway toward the double doors that led out back. The floors shone, the walls spotless. He took pride in keeping Barbara Jordan Elementary as clean as possible, and he would bet there wasn't a cleaner school in the whole state, if not the country.

He wheeled the cart through the doors into the mid-day heat, and turned toward the dumpster. The dumpster was like a crockpot under the sun, slow-cooking the garbage within. Some of the cafeteria workers were gathered there, smoking cigarettes, all speaking in Spanish, and Grady wondered how they could breathe the dumpster fumes in for so long. When they saw Grady, they looked almost nervous at first until they realized it was just the janitor.

"Guys, it's an elementary school. You can't smoke here."

They pretended like they couldn't understand him though he knew damn well they could. He decided to just let it go, tossed the bag containing the dusted vomit into the dumpster, then wheeled his cart back into the school.

Stomach grumbling, he parked the cart outside of the janitor's closet, and stepped through the door. The brown paper bag containing his bologna sandwich and red delicious apple sat on the shelf with the bottles of all-purpose cleaner. He snatched it, took a seat on a milk crate he'd nabbed a few months back, and bit into the sandwich, the mayonnaise overflowing onto his fingers. As he licked his fingers clean, he couldn't help but let Ms. Flowers enter his thoughts. The woman was in his head so often he could charge her rent.

She smiled at me today. She'll realize how madly in love she is with me one of these days.

Grady made quick work of his lunch, used a moist wipe to clean his hands and face, then wheeled his cart toward the cafeteria. There was still an hour before the kids would have lunch, but he figured he'd get there early, sweep the floors, wipe down the tables before they got there. He knew the cafeteria workers wouldn't care enough to do it.

And Ms. Flowers will be there.

He packed his cart up with rags, cleaner, and his broom and dustpan, then headed out of the janitor's closet, which served as his break room and office, and wheeled his cart down the hall toward the cafeteria.

He whistled as he strolled across the linoleum, slowing his pace as he passed Ms. Flowers's classroom. Terribly lascivious images spun through his mind then, and though he knew it was inappropriate to think this way in the presence of children, there wasn't anything he could do to stop them. Within his mind, Ms. Flowers loved him, wanted him. Had to have him.

Save it for home, Grady.

***

And save it he did. He wasn't in his apartment for more than a minute before he had found himself in the bathroom, standing over his toilet, splashing threads of pearly seed into the water as he imagined Ms. Flowers kissing him, on top of him, screaming his name.

Grady! Oh God, Grady!

Once he had finished, he flushed it down, leaned his forehead against the wall as he collected himself. The toilet seemed to choke as the water swirled down, going much slower than usual, just barely swallowing down his load. It was sort of depressing how often he had been finding himself in this position, and he thought that if his toilet could talk, it would call him pathetic.

He zipped up with a sigh, then headed for the sink to wash his hands. A stray pubic hair had somehow found itself pasted to the side of the sink by a glob of blue toothpaste, and Grady plucked it, let it swirl into the drain, then rubbed the toothpaste off with his thumb.

Now that his brain could think regular thoughts again, he took a long look at his toilet as he dried his hands, which was still making that choking sound. And something was off about its appearance. It wasn't until he studied it for a few seconds more that he realized it looked…fat. The bowl bulged out, but the porcelain didn't seem to be cracked anywhere. He wiped his hands on his pants as he walked over, bent at the knees, then ran his palms over it. It felt normal, and he was pretty damn sure porcelain couldn't get water damage and swell up.

Shit, this is just what I need.

Since money was tight, he figured maybe he could google this, try and fix it himself. As he trudged back down his hallway toward his bedroom, he thought back to the smile Ms. Flowers had given him. He wished he knew her first name, wished he knew what kinds of things she liked to do, what her favorite food or music was.

He hadn't been on a date in years, not since he had nearly drowned in his own depression.

Not since the razor blade dug trenches into his wrists, down his arms.

It wasn't until he really thought about it that he realized how lonely he was. He kept himself busy by sitting on his couch and watching TV, and though he'd been looking forward to the next episode of *The Jogging Dead* all day, the thought of sitting there alone, again, filled him with dread.

He forced Ms. Flowers' smiling face out of his head as he sat in front of his computer and wiggled the mouse to get rid of the screen saver. With his fingers on the keyboard and Google awaiting his command, he was stumped on what to type.

How to fix a toilet bowl bulge. Enter.

He didn't expect anything to come up for that search, not for that issue specifically anyway. But the very first item to pop up was an image, along with a link to a plumbing company's website. "Does your toilet look like this?" it said. The image was of a toilet, its bowl swollen and round just like his.

Why, yes it does, Grady thought as he clicked the link. He was surprised to find anything on bulging toilets since it was a phenomenon he had never heard of before. But the website had no instructions on what the problem could be and how to fix it. There was only a phone number.

"Figures," he said to himself. *The bastards want money.*

He left the website and went searching elsewhere, but couldn't find a single other post regarding the issue of overweight toilets.

After sitting there for at least an hour and getting nowhere, he decided to head back to the bathroom and take another look. Work at it with a plunger or something. *Maybe it's just something stuck down in there,* he thought, but knew that couldn't be the problem. What could make hard porcelain swell up like that?

The quiet of his apartment sent tremors of depression over his flesh, and he did his best to ignore it as he made his way back down the short hallway toward the bathroom. Dark thoughts began to surface, the kinds of thoughts he used to have before he got his job, the kind of thoughts that used to make his flesh crave sharp metal, or his stomach crave all the pills in his cupboard.

No, he thought. *That's not me anymore. Right?*

Hell no. He was just feeling lonely, he knew, and there was nothing abnormal about that. He had thought about maybe getting a dog a few times, but knew he could never go through with it. Not after...

He had a dog when he was a kid, might have been about ten or so. No matter how hard he thought about it, he couldn't remember the dog's name, couldn't remember the color or the breed. He only remembered its broken, squashed body

11

after the truck had rolled over it in the street just in front of his house. A small dog, he remembered that, because he had wondered how so much blood and guts could have possibly been held within such a tiny thing.

Ever since then, imagining himself being responsible for another life scared the hell out of him. He told himself he was just a kid then, that he had nothing to do with what happened, even though he was the one who threw the ball, he was the one who told the dog to go get it.

That dog trusted me. He trusted me and I let him die. I deserve to be alone.

Once he was back in the restroom, staring at the toilet's bulging bowl, all other thoughts were flushed from his mind. It looked almost as if the bulge had grown in the last hour.

"What the hell is wrong with you?" he said to the toilet as he retrieved the plunger from under the sink.

He stood over the toilet, plunger at the ready, and peered inside. Lodged at the bottom was something white and round, thin strands of what looked like blond hair drifted off its surface.

How did I not see that before?

Setting the plunger down, he dropped to his knees and got a closer look. The only thing his mind could come up with was that some kind of albino rat got itself stuck and drowned in there, and now its corpse was lodged at the bottom of his toilet.

He still didn't see how this explained the issue with the bowl, but for now, he was happy to have a problem he could solve. He jumped back to his feet, grabbed the plunger's wooden handle with both hands, and got to work. But no matter how hard he plunged, the damn thing wouldn't budge. And now the toilet wouldn't even flush.

At the school, he had to touch all manner of awful things almost on a daily basis. The kids were always getting sick, always shitting or pissing themselves, and it was up to him to clean up after them. So jamming his hands into his own toilet was no big deal. That is, until his fingertips made contact with the thing stuck at the bottom of the bowl.

12

Grady yanked his finger out of the water as if he had just touched an oven range. He didn't know what he had been expecting, but the fleshy texture of this thing freaked him out, sent electricity down his spinal cord. If it was a rat, first of all, he would think it would be covered with more fur. Unless it had been under water so long that the hair had washed away along with all pigment of the skin. Also, a rat's carcass, especially a water-bloated one, would be squishy.

The thing at the bottom of his toilet was hard. Its surface was fleshy, like skin, but when he pushed his finger onto it, it didn't give at all. Almost felt like…

A head.

But it couldn't be a head, that was just stupid. He took a few quick breaths, then stuck his hands back into the water, tried gripping the thing but couldn't get a hold on it. After a few more failed attempts, he went back to the plunger, but got nowhere, no matter how hard he churned.

Son of a bitch. Guess I'll be eating Ramen noodles for the next month.

He washed his hands, then made his way back to his bedroom where he pulled up the plumber's number and called. It only rang once.

"H-hello?" The voice sounded nervous, high-strung.

"Yes, I found your number on the internet. That picture you've got posted…well—"

"Your toilet? Is…is it…is it swollen? Like sticking out?"

"Right. I can't figure out what's wrong with it, never seen anything like it. There's something stuck down there, but I can't get my hands on it to get it out, and—"

"Don't touch it! You m-might hurt it. What's…" the man breathed rapidly for a few seconds, "what's your address? Give me your address! Please…p-lease."

"Jesus, settle down. It's not that big of a—"

"Yes it is! Yes it is…you don't understand. If you don't… if you don't hurry up…please. Give me your address and I'll fix this for you."

Grady pinched the bridge of his nose and contemplated hanging up on this guy. Just hearing the man speak was stressful enough, Grady didn't want to meet the guy. "How much is this going to cost?"

"Nothing. I won't ch-charge you. Okay? I just want to make sure everything is okay…we can't let anything happen to your…your, uh…just trust me. You have to trust me."

Grady rolled his eyes, but went ahead and gave his address. "If you get here and try to spring up any surprise charges, I'm not paying. Understood? Free is free, right? Hello? Heeeellooo, are you there?"

It wasn't until the phone rang again that Grady realized the plumber had already hung up, and the sudden ring tone made him flinch and nearly drop the cell. The Imperial March—Darth Vader's theme music—played, and there was only one number assigned to that ring tone.

"Hey, Ma."

"Happy birthday to me, I guess." Her voice was shaky, but Grady could tell she was only trying to sound like she'd been crying.

"Ah hell. Sorry, Ma. I've been busy, and—"

"Busy? Doing what, wiping shit off bathroom walls? You don't know busy until you have children of your own… but you won't ever know anything about that, will you? Damn near forty and not married. Who's ever heard of such a thing? Yeah, I bet you're just busy as hell. Well, it's been a shitty birthday if you were wondering. Thought I might as well call my son."

"Thanks. Our conversations always make me feel so great." Grady ran a finger over the scar tissue on his wrist, had to fight the urge to throw his phone against the wall.

"Don't be a smart ass. A mother is supposed to be hard on her son, don't you know that? That's why there's so many pussies in the world today, because parents aren't hard on their kids anymore." The woman chuckled, her smoker's cough seeming to get worse every year. "But then again, look at you. Guess I wasn't hard enough."

"So…yeah. Great talking to you. Happy birthday or whatever."

"I might live in another state, Grady, but it's still only an eight hour drive. Whether you like my company or not, I'm still your mother goddamnit, and you're still my only son. Be nice to see you one of these days."

Grady cupped his forehead and clenched his teeth. He was about to make up an excuse, not only to decline visiting, but to get the hell off the phone. The sound of her voice was like a dull chainsaw cutting his brain into jagged slices.

But the noise coming from his bathroom caught his attention. It was like a low growl, almost like thunder in the distance. He thought he might have felt a slight tremble in the floor.

He was vaguely aware of his mother going on and on about something or other, but he lowered the phone and put his ear to the air. The rumble strengthened, sounded angry, almost like an oncoming train, and then the floor shook so hard he had to grab onto the kitchen counter to keep from falling.

"Ma, I...I gotta go!"

"It's my birthday, goddamnit—"

Grady had just hung up when the explosion shook his entire apartment. A scream ripped from his throat as he dropped to the floor, covered his head with both arms.

The thunderous sound only lasted a few seconds, and as soon as it and the rumbling stopped, Grady could hear the water.

There was a pounding coming from his upstairs neighbor, as if to say he was making too much noise.

What the hell do you want me to do, asshole?

He rushed toward the restroom, and as he got closer, the carpet began to squish under his feet. Water gushed into the hallway, streaming over the bathroom floor like a flood. It sounded like a waterfall had somehow found its way into his restroom, and he hesitated before stepping in.

"Holy shit!"

Chapter Two

"Another one? Are you serious?" John shook his head as he waved the flies away from his dinner, then used his plasticware to cut a piece off the greenish-brown turd sitting on his plate, and popped the morsel into his mouth. This one was fresh, and hot after heating it up in the microwave, and it melted like butter over his tongue. He always loved when it had that green color, though he was the only one out of his siblings who did. "How are we gonna fit another one in this little house?" he said through a mouthful of partially chewed feces.

"He's right. We runnin' outta room up in here," Ernesto said. He ate his leftover spaghetti on the counter across the kitchen from the table where John and the other kids ate their dinner. Ernesto was young, maybe five or six years older than John.

John took a sip of his urine-aid, wiped his mouth on his forearm. He watched as Herb packed up his tools, the tall scrawny man clearly shaking with excitement. He always looked nervous, but he was so bad now that he was actually whimpering, and just watching him gather his things made John feel antsy.

"I…I don't care. They need us, you guys. We…we're the only ones that can help. So get, get over it already. I'll be back s-soon." And just like that, he ran out of the house and was driving down the driveway before anyone could stop him.

"Chingao," Ernesto said as he finished off his food and tossed his dishes in the sink.

"You gonna wash those?" John's dad, Gus, had a voice like the engine of an 18-wheeler with a cat stuck in the fan belt. He sat in his sagging recliner in the living room watching the football game, and turned his body just enough to get a look at Ernesto. "Cuz ain't one of us your goddamn mama."

"Yeah. Whatever, man." Ernesto sucked on his teeth as he faced the living room.

Rosie finished her bowl, licked the brown goop from her lips, then tossed her dish in the sink along with her father's. She ran to Ernesto and he scooped her up, then wrinkled his nose.

"Go wash your mouth out, mija."

"Okay," she said as he set her back down, but her eyes were on the large man across the house. She slowly walked by the living room, her eyes glued to Gus who was already on his feet and facing Ernesto, his face the color of raw beef. She reached into her pocket and pulled out her chrome butterfly knife, twirled it until the blade stuck straight up. "Don't talk to my dad like that, pendejo."

Ernesto chuckled as he pulled a beer from the refrigerator and popped the tab.

John finished his dinner, then shared a look with Lou, Herb's son, who sat beside him. Lou had finished his food a long time ago—always a fast eater—but the older boy remained at the table. It wasn't very often that Lou wasn't at John's side.

"You need to teach your daughter some respect," Gus said to Ernesto, spittle raining from his lips. "If you don't, then I will. I see that goddamn knife again, I'm takin' it and shovin' it up *your* ass."

Ernesto sipped his beer and smiled. "You won't touch my daughter. Bet on that."

Rosie still stood in the same spot, baring her teeth as she stared up at Gus. She quickly swung her eyes toward Ernesto, almost as if she were asking permission to use the knife on Gus, and Ernesto shook his head slightly, still keeping that smile on his face.

John envied Rosie and Ernesto for being so close. He could barely talk to his dad anymore, and Gus seemed disgusted at the very sight of him. Which used to bother John when he was younger, but now he couldn't care less. The man was a drunk and an asshole. Always made John feel like he was an inconvenience, always bitching about having to work long hours to provide for him.

As John stood from the table, Gus's eyes landed on him, but John avoided eye contact, elbowed Lou on the shoulder to get his attention.

"Let's go to our room," John signed. "Want to play Mario Brothers?"

Lou nodded enthusiastically, signed back. "Yes! I've been waiting all day."

Rosie slowly backed away from the living room, tossing her knife from hand to hand, snickering. For only being five years old, she was a little bad ass. John was glad to have her as a little sister.

Gus looked ready to pop from the pressure building in his head. The beer can in his fist was partially crushed, and amber liquid poured over his fingers and pitter-pattered onto the carpet.

"Where the hell you think you're goin', boy?" Gus reached out with his free hand and gripped John's shoulder. "Did I say you were excused?"

John shrugged off the massive hand, and though he felt like cowering under the large man's stare, he stood his ground, started sidestepping toward his bedroom. "I'm just going to my room to hang out with Lou. What's the big deal? You can sit here and watch your precious game, and us stupid kids won't be in your way."

Gus slammed the beer can to the floor and raised his fist. "You watch your goddamn mouth, boy! I'm your father, damnit, and I want the respect I deserve. From all of you sons of bitches. Work all goddamn day, put food in yer bellies. Shit!" His eyes jumped to Ernesto, then rolled back to John.

Lou whined beside John, signed the same thing over and over. "Stop fighting."

"Whatever, old man. Gotta give respect to earn it, you feel me?" Ernesto said, still standing across the room from Gus in the kitchen.

Gus shoved past John, nearly tossing him to the floor.

18

Gus had a big gut, but his chest and arms were thick and as hard as rock, and though Ernesto talked tough, when he saw the big man coming toward him, the smirk he'd been wearing all night melted right off his face.

"What was that, asshole?" Gus growled.

"Nothin', man. It's cool." Ernesto had both hands in the air now. "If we all gonna live here, don't you think we should get along and shit? Chill out, homie."

"I get along just fine…homie. I don't like being disrespected in my own house after a long day of work wading through shit and piss, you hear me?" Gus bared his teeth, the cords in his neck bulging, and stormed into the kitchen toward Ernesto. He had already gone through a twelve pack that night, which was light drinking for him, but enough to get his blood boiling.

Rapid footsteps across the living room. John barely had time to see her before Rosie had climbed Gus's back like a cat up a tree, her knife clamped between her teeth. Then the blade was pressed against Gus's throat.

"What the—" Gus started to flail, but when Rosie pressed harder, he stopped, curled his hands into fists that hung at his sides like boulders.

Rosie hissed and water spilled from her mouth and drenched Gus's shirt. "Daddy?" she said through clenched teeth.

"Let him go, mija. He ain't shit." Ernesto's smirk returned. "Right, Gus?"

Lou flushed his mouth over and over, jumping up and down. "Please stop," he signed. "We are family. Please stop."

John just watched. He had a strange urge to help his father, but even more so, he knew the man deserved this. Maybe it would teach him a lesson, but John knew that was wishful thinking. This would only serve to piss him off even more.

Sweat rolled down Gus's face, and though his skin became an even darker shade of maroon, he nodded his head. "I'm cool, okay? Get this little spic bitch off me."

Ernesto nodded and Rosie hopped down, her knife still

out in front of her as she backed away toward her dad. Ernesto gathered her into his arms, kissed her on the forehead, and they both headed to their bedroom, whispering and laughing to each other.

John knew he needed to get to his room quickly before Gus took out his anger on him, like he always did. "Come on, Lou. Let's go."

Lou clutched John's shirt sleeve, his eyes wide and locked on Gus.

Gus turned and looked about ready to say something, then just shook his head, wiped his palm across his throat and checked it for blood, which there was none. He stomped toward the fridge and pulled out a fresh beer.

Once they were in their room, John got Lou to help him push their dresser in front of the door, just in case Gus decided to make a late night ass kicking visit. The man had only ever put his hands on John once, and John could tell he felt damn sorry about it, but that didn't change anything. John felt a lot better once the dresser was pressed up against that door.

"We gotta get out of here, Lou. I hate that son of a bitch," John signed.

"He's your dad. You can't hate him."

"Well I do. Now let's play the game so I don't have to think about it."

Lou flushed his mouth to show his happiness, then fired up the Nintendo.

"You go ahead first, okay? I'll be Luigi this time."

Lou agreed with a clapping of his hands. John knew it would be a while before he got a turn. Lou was damn good at Super Mario Brothers, had beaten it about a thousand times.

John turned on his computer and logged on. He had a message waiting.

Prettygirl18: Hey, John. I'm bored. I miss you. Talk to me.

BigBadJohn: I miss you so bad. I wish I could come to you, get the hell away from my house. I hate it here. I don't think I can take this much longer.

Prettygirl18: What's keeping you?

Chapter Three

It was like a geyser, water gushing out of the toilet's bowl like an upside down waterfall. The water crashed against the ceiling, the walls, sprayed Grady and soaked him completely. He had to turn his head and breathe through his mouth to keep from drowning as he forced his way in to the bathroom to try and figure out a way to stop it.

Just as he reached the toilet, the water stopped, just shut off as if someone had hit a switch. He didn't realize he was screaming until the roaring sound of the water ceased, and he leaned against the wall and ran both hands through his dripping hair, gasped as he caught his breath.

Water was everywhere, dripping off every surface in the cramped bathroom. The bathtub was halfway filled with it, and the sink overflowed, sputtering as it drained

"Jesus…what in the hell… *Aarrgghh!*"

Grady's stomach suddenly twisted with pain, and he splashed to the floor and clutched his mid-section, grimacing and grunting. A gurgly cranking sound roared from his belly. He reached up to grab something—anything—so he could squeeze it as the pain rode his body, but ended up ripping the shower curtain down over himself. Everything went dark then, everything smelled like plastic.

Oh god…I'm about to shit myself.

He wanted to sit on the toilet and take care of the problem, but he was too scared another eruption would explode and burst his rectum. If the pain got any worse, he would just have to take the risk.

I've never had to shit so bad in my life.

Once the pain had subsided enough for him to move, he threw the curtain off of him and carefully got to his feet. He grabbed fistfuls of hair as he stared down at his toilet. The water eruption had closed the lid, and Grady wondered if the white hairy thing at the bottom of the toilet had been blown out like a cannonball.

He checked the floor, the sink, even let his eyes coast to the ceiling, but he didn't see anything but water, a few stray pubic hairs like curly spider's legs.

Using the big toe of his left foot, he nudged the lid back up, and took a peek inside. The thing was still down there, it had moved out further, but not far enough to see the rest of its body. It was just more of the white bulge, a light dusting of hair. The white flesh was crisscrossed with blue veins, and as Grady stared at it, he could have sworn they were pulsating slightly.

In the next second, the pain returned with a vengeance, hit him hard, grabbed hold of his guts and dug its nails in. He doubled over, peeled his lips past his teeth and shrieked. As the pain rolled through him, he could feel his bowels trying to release, every movement nearly making him lose control. He did everything he could to hold it in, didn't think he had the courage to sit on the exploding toilet with that pale...thing down there. He just knew as soon as he did, the creature would dislodge itself, and tunnel into him. A sound much like the thunder that had rumbled from the toilet gurgled from his belly, and he clutched it, groaned.

Oh Jesus please hurry!

He hoped the plumber wasn't too far, because if the guy didn't show up quick, Grady was going to take a squat in the bathtub and release the demons scraping their talons along his rectum.

The pain let up enough for him to catch his breath, and he just stood there, back against the wall, studying the object at the bottom of his toilet.

It has to be some kind of animal. Maybe this thing crawled up out of the sewer, drowned before it made it to the surface. And now it's stuck in my toilet.

But as he ogled it, he had no idea what species of animal this thing could be, wondered if it was some kind of mutation or something. Then he couldn't help but let his mind wander

22

to disease, and if this thing could possibly be infected with something. The water soaking every inch of him suddenly felt filthy, and he could feel the bacteria crawling across his flesh.

Knock knock knock.

The sound made Grady flinch, and he lost his footing, ran in place for a few seconds before slipping and crashing down onto his ass. He lay there for a minute, writhing and moaning. The collision with the floor had loosened his clutching buttocks muscles, just enough for a spurt of liquid shit to ooze out and soak into his boxer shorts.

"Oh god!"

Knock knock knock.

"I'm coming!"

He climbed to his feet, winced as the hot stew slid down his leg, but made his way across the soaked hallway carpet and opened the front door.

"Show me…show me the way. Qu-quickly," the plumber said as he stumbled his way inside. He nearly shoved Grady back to the floor as he forced his way into the house.

"Wait a minute, now. You can't just—"

"There's no time for this! I might…I might already be too late. Please, you have to…" The plumber squinted at Grady through thick glasses, his nose wrinkled and his front teeth showing up to his gums. The man looked Grady up and down, and only became more frantic. "Oh g-god…the water already broke! When? H-how long ago did it happen?"

Water broke? He must be talking about the pipes or something.

"It just happened a few minutes ago. There's this thing stuck at the bottom of the toilet, some kind of animal or something. Then the damn water just exploded, got everywhere. I've never seen anything like that before…and that thing is still stuck down there."

The plumber threw his hands in the air and whimpered as he clumsily sprinted into the living room, turning his head left and right.

"Down the hall," Grady said.

"H-hurry!" Water splashed out of the carpet as the scrawny man ran across it.

The plumber, maybe forty years give or take, looked like little more than a skeleton tightly wrapped in flesh-colored spandex. The man's glasses magnified his eyes to a ridiculous size, and he seemed incapable of unsquinting. His toolbelt looked like it weighed more than him, and the tools jingled as the plumber jogged. He grabbed the doorframe on either side of him and peered into the bathroom, then spun and faced Grady, who still stood in his place by the front door.

"Jesus Christ, will you come on! She's ready...she's ready!" Then he stepped in and disappeared from Grady's view.

Grady rushed over, wondering if he had just let a crazy person into his apartment, as if his night could possibly get any worse. At that moment, he wanted nothing more than to relieve the ever growing pressure in his stomach and take a shower to get the diseased water off of him. Just as the thought emerged into his mind, another surge of agony grabbed hold of his bowels and squeezed. He couldn't stop the scream and he found himself on his knees, his sweatpants soaking up the water in the carpet.

Grady's jaw ached from clenching his teeth so hard, and he slowly worked his way back to his feet, took steady and careful steps as he made his way to the restroom, afraid to wake the monster inside of him again.

When Grady finally stepped inside, the plumber was already on his knees in front of the toilet. He swirled his long, skinny hands over the toilet's bulge.

"She's ready," the man said. "I...I got here just...just in time." Without waiting another second, he reached one hand into the bowl, used the other to rattle the handle. "Hand me that...that plunger."

Grady did as the man asked, but smacked his lips. "You think I didn't try that already? I worked at that damn thing for hours. Won't do you any good."

But the plumber had no interest in anything Grady was saying. He glared into the toilet bowl, tongue clamped between his teeth as he worked the plunger a few times, then stuck both hands in and swirled them in a circular motion.

This went on for what felt like an hour, maybe more. Grady didn't know what else to do besides stand there and watch. And hold back his loosening bowels with every muscle in his body. He didn't know how much longer he could possibly hold it, and he danced in place, concentrated on his breathing, curled and uncurled his fists.

"I think I've got an emergency brewing over here, man. How much longer do you think—"

The man's mouth propped open, then widened even more into a smile. "Here we are. Come on now...m-my god she's beautiful."

"What?"

Then the plumber pulled his hands out of the toilet, and he was clutching something, stood up and cradled it.

"A g-girl...you've got yourself a girl." The man's eyes looked insane through the thickness of his glasses as he beamed down at the bundle in his arms. He held it out to Grady. "C-come say...come say hello."

It's that thing. He's got the dead animal in his arms...

That's when it started moving. Sort of flopped and writhed like a small white fish. And then a strange sound choked out of it.

Is it...is it crying?

The sound only grew in volume, sounded wet, almost like a toilet flushing. The thing wiggled, nearly thrashed right out of the plumber's arms. Its wails rose in intensity and pitch, and then it turned, locked eyes with Grady.

And the crying ceased at once. Its eyes—the most beautiful blue he'd ever seen—penetrated his own. Its skin was pure white, and wisps of wet blond hair clung to its little forehead. The bottom lip was wide and curved.

Like a toilet seat.

As Grady just stood there and stared at it, the strange little child got to wiggling again, whined and smacked its mouth. Its tongue was even bluer than its eyes—urinal cake blue.

25

Two things happened to Grady, almost simultaneously. First, he was filled with a love that he never knew he was capable of. He didn't know why a baby had been lodged at the bottom of his toilet, or how it could have possibly survived something like that, but now that he was looking at it, now that it was there in his bathroom, he wanted nothing more than to hold it, kiss it. Take care of it forever, regardless of its deformities or possible diseases.

The other thing he noticed was that his urge to shit went from emergency to code red.

"Oh jesus…can you please step out for a minute? I need to…I need—"

"You…you need to poop, I know. It's only natural. Paternal…paternal instincts. Happened to me too…it happened to all, all of us."

"What? Whatever, man, just step out for a minute and let me take care of it please." Grady hopped from foot to foot and clenched his teeth. Another couple of seconds and it would be too late.

"Don't blow it yet. You have to pull the cord first." The man held up the baby and thrust it gently toward Grady again.

The baby looked slippery, and the way it was wiggling made him nervous, so he shot his arms out and took hold of her to make sure she didn't fall. When he pulled her to his chest, he noticed the bronze chain protruding from her belly, the large black rubber float attached to the other end. The float was wrapped with pulsating veins that spread across the wet, black surface like tiny roots.

Just holding the baby caused his anus to open up momentarily, spurt a glob of liquid that ran down his leg. He winced, growled, shot a hard look at the plumber.

"Just what the hell am I supposed to do here? What's happening?" Grady looked back down at the baby, and his heart skipped a beat. She looked up at him, into him, and smiled. A soft coo burped from her lips, and she lifted both hands, ran her tiny little white fingers across his chin. Grady felt a tear forming at the corner of his eye, and he smiled back.

"She's your daughter. D-don't you see?"

"My daughter? I don't…that's impossible."

The plumber snickered and squinted hard. "Look, I can…I can explain the rest later. Right now, you need to feed her. Sh-she's hungry. Now pull that cord and…and let her eat."

Grady's legs shook as he clenched his muscles. He grabbed hold of the baby's bronze cord—it was soft like gummy worms. With a hard yank, it detached with a pop, left a perfect little hole in the baby's belly. She giggled, snuggled up into his chest.

"Now flush it. The toilet…the toilet's gonna need that to recuperate. The n-nutrients will help with the…with the healing."

Nothing coming out of his man's mouth was making any sense, and Grady thought he could feel his sanity start to dissolve. *I finally went nuts, that's what's happening. None of this is real.*

As Grady held the spongy chain, the venous, rubber float began to shrivel.

"H-hurry, man. Toss it in."

Grady did as he was told, flushed it down The chain and float swirled for a second before being sucked down and disappearing. The toilet seemed to sigh, and then everything became eerily quiet.

Until Grady's stomach reminded him he was about to explode.

"Can I shit now?"

"Yeah…yeah, of course." The plumber made his way toward the door, smiling and shaking his head.

"Well…could you hold her? Until I'm finished at least?"

"Hold her? I told you…she's hungry. Why do you think you have to go so b-bad? Like I said before, it's…it's paternal instinct. Your body was preparing for this, now drop that baby in the t-toilet and feed her."

It took Grady a second to let that sink in, to really understand what this man was telling him to do.

"That's…Jesus. That's messed up, man. You can't be serious."

27

"She's half toilet. W-what else did you think she'd eat?" He chuckled, pulled his drooping toolbelt up. "Now feed her. They can get real f-fussy when they're hungry."

And with that, the plumber stepped out of the restroom, shut the door behind him.

"Whoa…whoa," Grady said as the baby grabbed hold of his shirt and started trying to climb out of his arms. She crawled her way onto his shoulder, then clutched the fabric on the back of his shirt.

She's trying to get to my backside. She can smell it.

"Oh my god, are you kidding me?"

With a sigh, Grady pried the baby off his back, placed her gently into the toilet bowl. She cooed and splashed around, then tilted her head back and opened her mouth as wide as it would go. The fluorescent light gleamed off her lower lip.

As he stood there, staring at the baby, he realized how much she looked like her mother. And in that moment, it dawned on him what was happening. It didn't seem possible, but he knew it to be true, was as certain about it as he was certain he was about to fill his pants with hot, fresh feces.

Can I do this? Can I really shit into a newborn's mouth?

A violent tremor shook his legs and back, and he quickly dropped his pants and sat down.

The baby's lips pressed up against him, latched on like a vacuum nozzle. The upper lip was soft and fleshy, but the lower lip felt as hard as the toilet seat he now sat upon.

As he let loose, he sighed simultaneously with relief and disgust. The baby splashed around as it ate, and a high-pitched whine rattled out from Grady's lips.

I'm a daddy. What the hell am I supposed to do now?

***

"What? What do you mean?" Lou followed John around the room, splashing water all over the place.

John sighed, stopped packing his bag long enough to face his brother. Though they all had different parents, they considered each other siblings, and John wasn't sure if there were any other people like them anywhere in the world.

"I can't stay here anymore," he signed to Lou who was already shaking his head and wobbling his bottom lip.

"Please don't leave. You can't leave me here." Blue tears ran down Lou's hard, white face. One of his eyes was larger than the other, the smaller one always a pink color, always crusted over. Water spilled out of his mouth as he began to weep. Lou was older than John by a few years, but had the mind of a child. John always watched out for him, felt bad that he had to leave him behind, but he knew he had to, knew that if he didn't do this now he might never go through with it. He had one chance at happiness and he was going to take it.

"I'm sorry. I'll miss you…I'll miss Rosie too. But there's a girl out there who loves me. And I love her."

Lou wouldn't look John in the face anymore, just stared at his hands as he signed. "Who is she? Is she like us?"

"No. She's normal. I've only talked to her online, but she really likes me. Look." John pulled Lou toward the computer where he opened up his account, double-clicked on Prettygirl18's profile. A picture of a young girl popped up, puckering her lips, clad in a white bikini top that did little to hide her breasts.

"Wow. She's really pretty," Lou signed, then wiped the tears from his face.

"Right? We're going to get married one day. She loves me, Lou."

"Did you tell her what we are?"

John ignored the question as he went back to packing. No, he had not. But he was convinced that once she met him, it wouldn't matter. By then, she would already love him for *who* he was, not *what* he was.

Lou grabbed hold of John's arm and spun him around. "You haven't told her, have you? Don't leave, John. Please."

John set his bag on his bed and sat down, waved Lou over to sit with him. "Are you happy here? I mean…really happy?"

Lou shrugged. "I love my dad."

29

"You're lucky. My dad's an asshole," John said as he stuck his middle finger up at the wall that separated his room from the living room. "They keep us here like we're freaks or something. I can't take it anymore, Lou. I wanna see what else is out there. I wanna know what it feels like to kiss a girl. Don't you?"

Lou shook his head. "No."

John ran his hand over the small tuft of black hair at the top of his head. He caught his reflection in the television screen and studied it for a minute.

What if she sees me and freaks out? What if I disgust her?

John's face was almost human from the nose up, but his mouth stuck out like a duck's bill, his upper and lower lips like the lid and seat of a toilet. Small round teeth lined his purple gums, and his dark blue tongue lay at the bottom of an ever-present pool of water in his mouth. He stared at his bleach-white hands, hardened them into fists.

No. She'll love me. Once she gets to know me, she won't be able to help it.

John had already decided to try and eat normal food once he met up with his Prettygirl18. At least at first he would. He didn't think any girl—a normal girl—would want to kiss someone who just ate crap. To John, it smelled fantastic, tasted even better, but he knew normal people didn't feel the same way about it. His dad had told him how disgusting it was countless times, and he'd even caught Uncle Herb and Ernesto wrinkling their noses. He had tried to eat normal food before, but couldn't hold it down, ended up throwing up into his mom and crying on the bathroom floor as his stomach twisted itself into knots.

I can get used to it. I'll be fine.

"The world is scary," Lou signed. "My dad says people are mean."

"Not all people. Not everyone can be mean. Our dads are just scared something will happen to us, but I'd rather take that chance than stay locked up in this house for the rest of my life. I'm sixteen, Lou. You're even older than me. There has to be more for us out there. There has to be."

Lou was slumped over. He looked almost exactly like a toilet, but had stubby arms and legs sticking out of him. He had no ears, just a flush handle on one side, which he pulled to flush his mouth when he was happy. Now, the water overflowed from his mouth, soaked the comforter, but John didn't mind. He would be gone in a matter of a few hours, was just waiting to make sure everyone was asleep first.

"I'm sorry, Lou. I'll come back for you. One day, once I'm settled into my new life, I'll come back and get you and you can come live with me. Okay?"

Lou didn't answer, wasn't even looking at John as he was signing.

John was going to miss his brother. He was going to miss Rosie too, even though she could be a handful. She was the youngest but easily the alpha kid in the house. She almost looked like a normal girl, but her head was a square shape, and her bottom lip was soft and padded and covered in a floral pattern. Her skin had a slight bluish hue to it, just like her mom.

Their mothers, all three of them, were installed into the large bathroom at the end of the hall. John spent time with his mom every day, just sitting next to her, talking to her. He would miss her most of all.

The sudden pounding on the door startled them both.

"John? J-John...please. I'm sorry. Okay? I don't mean to be...like this."

Oh god, he's a sad drunk tonight.

John hated these nights even worse than when Gus was an angry drunk. When he was angry, he'd throw some things around, cuss a lot, and then eventually pass out. The sad nights seemed to last forever.

"Go away, Dad. I'm not in the mood for this tonight."

The knob turned, but the door slammed against the dresser they had pushed in front of it. His dad's fingers snaked in, but that was all he could manage to fit through.

"Come on, John. I'm your d-dad, goddamnit. Let me in...I, I wanna talk to ya."

"No. Go to sleep. It's late."

Slam! "Open this fuckin' door!"

"Just let him in," Lou signed.

John shook his head, crossed his arms. He fought the tears, held them back as best he could, but one snuck by, rolled down his cheek.

John stared at the window beside his computer, thought about just climbing out now and leaving. But he needed his dad's car keys, and while the drunk bastard was awake, he knew there was no chance of getting them without fighting for them. And as pissed as he was at the man, he had no intention of fighting him.

"I hate you," John said.

The pounding stopped and the fingers reappeared, but only for a moment before they were pulled away again. John thought he heard some sniffling, then retreating footsteps.

I can't wait to get the hell out of here.

Chapter Four

When Grady had finished, he stood up off the toilet seat, turned and peered into the bowl.

Empty.

At first, he thought the whole thing had been some kind of strange dream, and he was filled with more disappointment than relief. But he could feel something hanging off his backside. With his back to the mirror, he lifted up on his toes, and there she was, fast asleep but still clinging to him with her mouth. Her body hung loose, feet kicking lightly as if she was having a dream about riding a bike.

Grady couldn't reach her by twisting, and had to bend over, reach under his legs with both hands, and pop her off. Her suction was so good, he was scared she'd pull his asshole inside out. He ripped off a couple of squares of toilet paper and wiped her mouth. There wasn't much mess, but just a slight little brown dribble. Next, he wiped himself, steadying the child in his other arm. The paper came away clean, though his legs were striped with brown crust.

She ate every drop.

The baby whimpered, smacked her mouth. Runny saliva poured from between her lips in a constant trickle, and he used his shirt to wipe it up again and again.

His eyes rolled toward the toilet. The toilet he had squirt all manner of awful things into throughout the years. The toilet he had leaned up against when he slid the razor blade across his wrists. He felt bad for a second, realizing how abusive he'd been to his daughter's mother all these years, but then he realized he had only been feeding it. He started to feel embarrassed for all the times he had stood over it, Ms. Flowers in his mind, fingers wrapped around himself.

God, the toilet must think I'm some kind of pervert.

33

"Sorry about that," he whispered, running his fingertips over the baby's soft, blond hair. "But hey, if I didn't do it… we wouldn't have this little angel, now would we?"

There was a slight hiss and the water rippled a bit.

It was then that Grady remembered the plumber out in his living room. If the guy even bothered to stick around.

Grady was going to call out for him, but he didn't want to wake the baby. He grimaced as he pulled his soiled britches back up. He thought about jumping in the shower fist, but he had questions, and the plumber seemed to know what was going on here.

He crept across the soaked carpet, scared to move too quickly and jostle the sleeping toilet baby. Her skin was so white, sparkling in the dim lighting of the tiny apartment. An apartment so small, he couldn't imagine raising a child there.

But I can't leave. I can't ever leave. Her mother is here.

The plumber sat on the couch, tapping his long fingers on his knees nervously, and when he saw Grady walk in he jumped to his feet, nodded his head and grinned so hard his glasses slipped down the bridge of his nose.

"All b-better? How is she?" His eyes coasted to the baby and he clapped his hands, held them over his mouth. Fat tears rolled down his face and he whimpered slightly. "I'm…I'm sorry. I always get like this when…I get emotional when they're born."

"You keep saying they. Who's they? Are there more… um…?"

"Toilet babies. I know the name sounds c-cruel, but that's what we call them." The plumber reached into his back pocket and pulled out his wallet, flipped it open. "That's my…my son. Lou. He definitely looks more like his m-mother."

At first, Grady thought he was looking at a photograph of a regular toilet. But then he noticed the eyes, one much larger than the other. The child looked like his body was just a giant toilet head, his arms sticking out of where his ears should be, legs sticking out under his chin.

"Me and Lou…we live outside of the city. Got a s-small house I built when…when Lou was a toddler. Didn't want

34

anyone to see him…because I was scared. Scared of what they'd do to him." He flipped the wallet to another picture, this one of a group of men, each one of them with a child. All toilet children. "This is the rest of the f-family. We all live together in that house now…all of us have toilet babies."

"How did you guys find each other? I randomly found you on the internet. Doesn't that seem odd?" Grady stared at his daughter and couldn't hold back his smile. "Why aren't there more toilet babies out there? I mean…now that I know how they're made, why haven't I ever heard of this before? I figure there's gotta be lots of guys that use their toilets for… you know…"

The plumber shrugged. "Don't know. Maybe there are and they're kept secret, kind of like our kids. W-we just sort of…found each other. I…I don't know how it works. It's like…like we were m-meant to find each other. To be together." The plumber sniffled, pulled his thick glasses off his face long enough to wipe his eyes, which looked like tiny pinpricks without the glasses, then offered his hand. "I'm Herb by the way."

Grady extended a hand as far as he could without disturbing the baby, and Herb shook it lightly. "Grady. It's nice to… How is this possible?"

Herb smiled, his eyebrows raising and nearly touching his hairline. "Well…y-you busted one too many nuts into your toilet. It's really as…as simple as that."

Grady's face burned red and he opened his mouth to plead his case.

Herb held up a hand and flicked his eyelids. "Don't worry. That's how it happened to all of us."

"This is crazy…this is just... This is crazy." Grady still wasn't convinced this entire thing wasn't some kind of dream, and that he would wake up any minute on his couch, the side of his face pasted to the cushion by saliva, the TV playing infomercials and casting multi-colored light onto the walls.

"It's not c-crazy. It's a miracle. You're a dad now. H-how do you feel?"

35

The baby turned, sighed sweetly, rolled her head against the softness of Grady's chest. As he stared at her, as the tears continued to stream down his face, all fears he had about being responsible for another life faded away. He wasn't scared anymore. This wasn't a dog, this was his daughter. And he was determined to give her a good life, to make sure she was as happy as any child in the world. His chest throbbed with a kind of love that he had never felt before, and it felt damn good to love something so much, with every cell in his body.

"I feel amazing." He wiped his face. "But I still have so many questions."

Herb nodded. "Of course...of course you do. But before we get into all th-that...what's her name?"

Grady lifted her and planted a light, gentle kiss on her downy, white forehead. "Patty. I'm gonna call her Patty."

He didn't know why, but the name just seemed right. As if in response, a tiny smile arched the baby's mouth and a string of drool oozed over her porcelain lip and soaked into Grady's shirt.

"Patty. That's a p-pretty name." Herb still had his wallet out, and he started pointing out the men and children. "That's me and Lou there, when Lou was about fourteen. He's nineteen now, can you...can you believe that? It goes by so f-fast. That's Gus and John there. John's sixteen now, and k-kind of a drama queen. But that's to be expected with teen...teenagers. Not my Lou, though. He's a s-special boy." Herb adjusted his glasses and cleared his throat. "And that's E-Ernesto and Rosie. This was taken the day they joined the family, and R-Rosie was the youngest...until now."

The men and kids all looked happy. "That's great that you guys have each other. The kids must love being around others...like themselves."

"We want you to come and...come and live with us, Grady. You and P-Patty."

"What? I...I can't. I mean...really?"

Herb put his wallet back in his pocket, adjusted his toolbelt. "Of course. We have to...have to look out for each other. I told you…we find each other. It was m-meant to be."

Grady looked around his apartment again and realized quickly that he wouldn't miss it. "What about Patty's mom? I can't just leave her here. It doesn't seem right."

"No, no. Of course not. I'll bring her w-with us. That's why I b-brought my tools." He grinned and patted his belt. "Won't take that long. Even b-brought a replacement with me just in…just in case."

Grady was about to make the argument that he needed time to gather his things, to clean up, but his eyes coasted back to Patty as she gurgled and kicked her legs, and he swallowed the words. "Yes. You're right. We'll come with you."

"I knew you…you'd say yes. I told you…this was supposed to h-happen. Welcome to the f-family, you guys." Herb circled around behind Grady and hugged him. The man laid his head on the back of Grady's neck, had his arms wrapped around Grady's stomach.

"Um…thank you." Grady wanted to wiggle free, but he could hear the man weeping slightly, and he decided to just let it be. The guy was bringing him and Patty to his home, welcoming them into his family. Grady figured it wouldn't hurt to let the skinny man spoon him for a few seconds if that made him feel better. "Are you sure the others will be okay with this?"

Herb finally detached himself, walked back around so he could face Grady. "It'll be fine. They were all in this…in this position before. They know how hard it can be."

Grady nodded. "Thank you. Thank you so much."

"Why don't you p-pack up some clothes. I'll get started on Patty's…Patty's mama."

***

The ride to the house took about a half hour. Grady didn't realize how long it had been since he had left the city, and now that he was outside of it, away from all the concrete, glass, and lights, it felt damn good. Trees surrounded them now, and everything was so quiet. He felt like he could breathe better, could think more clearly. Hell, out there, he could see the stars.

Herb had a baby seat in his car, which Patty was strapped into, her head tilted to the side as she slept. Grady had asked about getting her some diapers, some clothing, and whatever else one needs to take care of a baby.

"Don't worry. We've got everything...everything you'll need at the house. Plenty of l-leftover diapers, which I specially made, and Patty can wear Rosie's old c-clothes."

Specially made diapers? Grady figured he'd ask later.

Grady had packed up his favorite clothes, which consisted of four different pairs of jeans and five shirts. Most of his underwear were thinned out and full of holes, but he grabbed the ones in the best shape, same with his socks. He only owned one pair of shoes, and didn't have a car. So he had packed light, was told by Herb that if there was anything he needed, the guys at the house could help.

Grady was grateful but couldn't help but feel uncomfortable depending on people he had never met before.

"You're sure everyone is going to be okay with this?" Grady checked over his shoulder to make sure Patty was okay. The baby gurgled and mewed, but was still fast asleep.

"Don't w-worry. They'll be so happy to meet you. And... and Patty. Lou is a great b-big brother."

They pulled down a dirt road that Grady would have missed if driving by, especially in the dark. There was nothing to mark it, and he figured that was on purpose. The road was just wide enough for Herb's sedan, fat tree trunks inches from scraping either side as they crept further into the darkness. The headlights were nearly swallowed whole by the night, illuminating nothing but gravel and trees. And then suddenly everything opened up. The house sat in the center of a small clearing, the forest surrounding the lot like a wooden force field. The house didn't look big enough to hold all of the people Grady had seen in the photograph in Herb's wallet.

A beat-up pickup truck sat alone in the gravel driveway, and Herb pulled the car in beside it, killed the engine. Just before the headlights were extinguished, Grady caught a face—as white as porcelain—in the driver's seat of the pickup. It ducked down quickly, and before Grady could say anything about it, Herb turned in his seat and smiled wide at Grady.

"Here we are, Grady. Welcome…welcome to your new home."

"Who's that?" Grady said, pointing through the windshield toward the truck.

"W-what?"

"I saw someone in the truck." Just then, there was a small whining sound, a few gurgles, then Patty was wailing.

* * *

"Shit." John had completely forgotten about Uncle Herb going out to help with the birth of another toilet baby. John knew he should be happy that another of his kind was being born, should be happy to get a new baby brother or sister, but he couldn't help but be annoyed. They didn't have room for anyone else in the house, and he had his own problems to deal with. Didn't have time to help care for a newborn, didn't have time to show some new guy how to raise a toilet baby.

Not that it matters anymore. I'm outta here first chance I get.

But he knew he'd been caught. The man sitting in the front passenger seat had locked eyes with John before he could drop out of view. And now that goddamn baby was crying, screaming her face off. It was only a matter of minutes before everyone in the house was outside. And John's plans were totally screwed.

He opened the truck door and stepped out, waved at Uncle Herb who was already out of his car, holding a big wrench with both hands like it was a broad sword. When he saw John, the terrified look on his face slackened and hung from his skull. He pushed his glasses up his nose and squinted.

"John? Y-you scared the hell out of me. Don't you…

39

don't you know I could have bashed your face in? Smashed your porcelain?"

John forced a smile. "I know, I know. I'm sorry. I thought I left my iPod in my dad's truck, and I was just out here looking for it. Didn't find it though."

The front door opened, and John turned to find Ernesto standing there, rubbing his eyes. Rosie stood next to him doing the same, and they both looked pissed for being woken up. Just behind them, Lou stepped out, and when he saw his dad, he flushed his mouth, then ran across the driveway into the man's arms.

John tried to lock eyes with his older brother, but Lou wouldn't look at him. He wanted to make sure Lou didn't say anything about his plans. Lou hated the idea of John leaving, and when John told him he was leaving tonight, he thought their entire bedroom would be soaked with toilet water before Lou was done throwing a fit. And Lou was really close to his dad, and John had a bad feeling Lou was about to spill the beans. If telling on John kept him there, kept him home, he figured Lou would do just that.

And John couldn't even blame him. Out there, all they had was each other, and John knew Lou looked up to him, even though Lou was the oldest. It would suck to have your best friend leave you just like that, but John had his mind made up. This had to happen, and it had to happen now.

The new man stepped out of the car, gave everyone a quick wave before throwing the rear passenger door open, which only intensified the volume of the baby's cries. They were so loud and so high-pitched that birds burst from the treetops and swarmed the night sky, cawing their disapproval.

But once the new man had the bay in his arms, it quieted down some. Still whimpered, still whined, but wasn't screaming anymore.

"It's hungry, homie," Ernesto said.

"Is it a girl?" Rosie's face suddenly lit up and her flowery lip pulled into a wide smile. "I hope it's a girl...cuz I'm sick of boys. Is it a girl, is it? Am I big sister?"

The new guy smiled and nodded, and Rosie started

jumping and clapping. It was the girliest John had ever seen her act.

"Everyone…this is Grady. He just had a. .had a baby tonight. Yes, Rosie. You…you're a big sister now. This is P-Patty."

Lou grabbed Uncle Herb's pant leg and pulled on it. Uncle Herb tried to shoo him away, but Lou was insistent, pointed toward John.

No, damn it. Don't say anything Lou…please!

"Lou, stop it. Don't be rude…say hello to your n-new uncle."

Lou stomped his foot, splashed water into the dirt. He turned and saw that John was staring at him. John widened his eyes and lightly shook his head. Lou signed, "You can't leave. You can't."

Quickly, John signed back, "Okay, okay. Just be quiet about it."

Lou smiled, flushed his mouth, and nodded. John rolled his eyes.

I can't tell Lou anymore about this. He'll ruin everything for sure.

"Hey, everyone. Sorry to wake you," the new guy said. "I'm Grady. Herb told me so much about you guys, I—"

The front door flew open and slammed against the house.

"What in the fuck is goin' on out here?" Gus stood in the doorway wearing nothing but some tight-fitting briefs. One hand picked at his belly button while the other massaged his forehead. "What's with all the goddamn noise? You have any idea what time it is…what time I gotta get my ass up in the mornin' to provide for this goddamn family?"

"G-Gus…watch your language, will you? We have…we have some new members to the family." Uncle Herb was now rubbing Lou's back who clutched his dad's leg with both hands.

The new guy, Grady, bounced from foot to foot as he tried to comfort the baby, but his eyes were on Gus, and he kept licking his lips, kept shooting nervous glances toward Uncle Herb.

John turned to look at his dad who still had a hand over his eyes as he tried to massage his hangover away. "Dad, we've got another baby. Her name's Patty."

Gus moved his hand, but only one eye was open. The other was pinched shut and surrounded by deep lines. He snorted, spat the wad of yellow phlegm into the dirt. "And what...they stayin' here, I take it?"

Herb stepped forward. "Yes, that's right. It's m-my house. And just like I helped you, just like I h-helped Ernesto...I'm gonna help Grady. Because...because we need each other. We were supposed—"

"If you start gettin' into all that destiny, 'we belong together' crap, I'm gonna hang myself, I swear to god."

John looked from his dad to the new guy, who had backed away from the house a few feet. The baby started to cry again, and John felt bad for Grady who looked completely lost.

"Shut that baby up, goddamnit." Gus had both eyes open now, but they were still squinted.

"Wait a minute, now. I know it's late, and I know you don't know me," Grady said, shouting over Patty's bawling. "But if you don't cool it, we've got problems. I'm not a violent man, but I've never had anything to fight for...until now."

There was a collective gasp, except for Ernesto and Rosie who laughed under their breath as they elbowed each other. Those two always seemed like they had some inside joke nobody else knew about.

John thought for sure that his dad was about to do something stupid. On his worst night, he had put his hands on John, hit him and kicked him after he'd fallen. Even went into the bathroom and kicked John's mom, broke her lid against the wall. After that, he had never hit John again, but his drinking got worse, and he grew more distant. He was even pissing in the yard now, as if he couldn't take facing John's mom again. That night, he had this certain look in his eye, a look that John still had nightmares about, a look that said he was about to cause some pain, show no mercy.

He had that look now as he stared Grady down.

Oh shit. I should grab the baby now before she gets hurt.

But Gus only spat in the dirt again, grunted once, then retreated back into the house. It seemed everyone breathed easier then, except for Ernesto and Rosie who still had smirks on their faces as if they were watching a TV drama or something.

John just felt embarrassed. He couldn't look Grady in the eye. "Sorry about my dad. He's just—"

"He's just an asshole," Rosie said, then elbowed Ernesto in the leg, but he smacked the back of her head and hissed.

"Watch your mouth, mija." He gave John a nod, which John found out was his way of trying to be friendly.

"Sorry." Rosie pouted for another second before the smile returned, and she darted across the driveway toward Grady. "Can I see her? Can I see the baby?"

"I think…I think she's hungry. Grady, let me sh-show you to the restroom. You still have…still have something left to give her?" Herb rubbed his belly as he said it. "And we're gonna want to put a diaper on her soon. You think our poop stinks? Just wait…wait til you smell hers." He sort of chuckled and adjusted his glasses. "But don't let any of it t-touch you. Burns like acid. That's why I had to customize the diapers, coat them with polypropylene so they wouldn't dissolve."

Having enough of the drama, John decided he needed to jump back online, let Prettygirl18 know that their rendezvous was going to have to be postponed for now.

But I still have the keys. It'll only be delayed a few hours. See you tonight, my love.

Chapter Five

Herb showed Grady into the house and led him to the bathroom, which Herb told him was the biggest room in the house. It had double doors, each with golden handles. Gold colored anyway, but they still looked nice.

"You can use E-Esmerelda," Herb said and pointed to the large toilet all the way to the left. "That's…that's Lou's mom. This one here is Guadalupe, Rosie's mom. And that one…that one's John's mom. Her name's Gwen, but don't say that in f-front of Gus. He thinks naming the toilets is…is stupid. So me and John n-named her." Herb had both hands on his hips as his head swept from left to right and back again, admiring the "ladies."

What struck Grady as strange was he could actually see a resemblance from these toilets to the kids they had birthed. Before, he never really noticed the differences in toilets, just did what he had to do into them, didn't concentrate on them long enough to admire them. Esmerelda was the largest, looked strong and sturdy. She had a bronze flush handle, the same as Lou. If she were to sprout arms and legs right then, she would look exactly like her son.

Guadalupe was a pale blue color, her seat puffy and padded, the kind that squealed and deflated when you sat on them. Rosie had the exact same seat for her lower lip, had the same blue color.

But when Grady studied Gwen, he couldn't really notice that much of a resemblance with John. Nothing that jumped out at him, anyway. He didn't really have a chance to compare Patty to her mother, but one thing he had noticed right away…

She has my eyes. The exact same.

"Esmerelda would l-love to help, isn't that right?"

It took Grady a second to realize Herb was talking to the toilet, but it hissed as if in response.

"She's all…all ready for you guys. When you're done f-feeding the baby…I'll show you to your room." Herb started out the door, and Grady had already set Patty in the water, already had his pants down to his knees when Herb turned back around with his finger pointed toward the space to the far right of the room. "And I'll get Patty's mother in-installed tonight. Don't want to keep them out of the…out of the ground too long. Especially when they're healing."

"Okay. Thanks, Herb."

Patty splashed around in the water, swimming in circles as she reached up for Grady's "feed hole." High-pitched whines burped out of her mouth, and the second Grady sat, she latched on. Her hard lips clamped down a little too hard, and Grady wiggled in his seat, groaned through clenched teeth, but he could do nothing to loosen her, and before he knew it, his bowels were already responding.

It hurt at first, and Grady didn't know if he would ever get used to it. But once he got going, the discomfort eased up a bit. He had to wonder how the guys were able to keep the kids fed. Of course, he didn't know how often he was supposed to feed them, but if it was any more than two or three times a day, he wasn't sure he had enough to give her.

And I don't know if I'd be comfortable letting Patty feed off the other guys. In fact, there's no way I could let that happen.

There was a slight vibration in the toilet seat, and Esmerelda hissed again. Grady couldn't help but wonder if she was trying to communicate with him, and just as the thought entered his mind, the other two toilets seemed to gurgle their water.

"Hey, ladies. I'm Grady. Nice to meet you." He felt stupid for talking to them, but it was something he knew he'd have to get used to. *The mother of my child is a toilet. Is it so farfetched that they can talk with me? At least understand me?* "This is Patty. Just born a few hours ago. Um…thank you girls for letting us stay here in your home."

They didn't respond, but Grady could tell they were pleased. The energy in the room was positive, and Grady smiled, tapped a tune onto his knees as he waited for Patty to finish. After another ten minutes or so, he felt her detach, and then heard her splash into the water. Grady wiped himself, though again it came away completely clean, then pulled his pants back up, and peered into Esmerelda's bowl.

He just couldn't believe how beautiful his daughter was. *God, if my mother knew I was a father, she would probably have a stroke.*

Not that he was in a hurry to tell the old hag. She had told him long ago that if he ever married a black or Mexican, she would disown him. She actually told him that the offspring would be an abomination. He had told himself back then that she was just old school, that it wasn't her fault for thinking that way. He knew now that she was just a bitter old witch, a person unable to be happy for another's happiness.

And if Grady told her that he squirt his seed into a toilet, and out popped a baby, she would probably tell him to kill it.

A fat tear formed at the corner of his eye, then splashed into the water just beside Patty's face. She lay on her back, floating, arms and legs spread out like a starfish. Tiny bubbles formed and popped at her mouth, and she had the slightest smile on her white lips.

Now that Patty was fed and not screaming in his ear, clutching at his shirt, his mind went back to his confrontation with the large man. Gus, he thought they had called him. Even though the others didn't seem quite as excited about Grady and Patty joining the family as Herb had let on, they didn't worry Grady, didn't come off as a threat the way Gus did. Grady was not a confrontational man, in fact, had spent most of his life avoiding it. But now that he was a father, something was different, something he couldn't explain. Even a monster of a man like Gus didn't scare Grady anymore, and if the big sonofabitch tried anything or said anything toward Patty, Grady knew he would have no problem defending her, physically if necessary.

I'll give him the benefit of the doubt for now. It's late, he was asleep. Maybe he was just grumpy.

Just as Grady was about to pull Patty from the water, the double doors creaked open. Herb's magnified eyes poked in, and Grady couldn't help but laugh, then waved the man in.

"How…how is she?"

"Passed out. This girl can eat."

Herb chuckled. "They…they eat a lot. That's one of the main r-reasons we need each other. To keep…keep them fed."

"No offense, Herb. But I don't think I can let you guys feed her. It just seems…it seems wrong. It still doesn't even feel right when I do it, you know?"

Lou waddled into the bathroom right as Herb began laughing. The skinny man patted Grady on the back and shook his head.

"No, she won't latch…latch on or anything. You'll spoon feed her. And not just from us…but with what G-Gus brings home from work. That's how we've kept all the kids f-fed all these years."

Lou had made his way to his mother, and beamed down at Patty. He turned his entire body in order to look at Grady, and it was hard to tell, but Grady was sure the kid was smiling. Then his hands started to move, quickly signing something, and when he was done, he reached up and pulled his flush handle. There was a loud whoosh from inside of his mouth.

"Lou says that Patty is adorable. He's excited to be her…be her big brother." Herb stepped forward and placed a gentle hand on his son's head. "My boy's deaf and mute. Doesn't have any…any ears or a tongue. That's why we all l-learned sign language."

Grady didn't know what else to do, so he gave Lou a thumbs up. The boy seemed to understand that just fine, and he stepped forward and hugged Grady's leg.

"He likes you. Lou's a very…a very sweet boy."

Grady just stood there and allowed the boy to hug his leg, and when he finally detached, stepped away with another flush of his mouth, Grady said, "You say you guys eat what Gus brings home. Where does he work?"

"In the s-sewers. He cleans them. Brings home b-buckets of food for the kids. It's the only way without having to take them…take them out of the house looking for food."

Lou was back at Esmerelda's side, gripping the bowl and peering into it.

"Lou's the oldest, right? How'd you keep him fed all by yourself?"

Herb adjusted his glasses and sighed. "Port-o-potties. Had to use them…use them like water wells. Whenever I saw one…I'd just l-lower a couple of buckets down there, take it h-home for Lou. Nasty work. Thanks to G-Gus, we don't have to do that anymore."

"Jesus." *So the asshole in the house is responsible for feeding the kids. That's just great.*

"W-we still feed them from ourselves, try and give… give them a fresh meal at least once a day. But we have to keep the ladies fed too. And no matter how much we all e-eat, there's just not enough."

Grady was still uneasy about Patty eating feces that came from anyone but himself, but if it came down to her eating the "sewer food" or going hungry, he figured he'd just have to get used to the idea.

"Why don't you help me haul in Patty's mama. I'll get her…get her installed tonight for you."

They pulled her out of the back seat of the car, and walked her back toward the bathroom. It looked like there was a spot reserved for her, just beside Guadalupe. As if Herb had known all along that they'd be coming, and at this point, Grady wouldn't doubt if that was exactly it.

Grady had offered to help, but Herb waved him off.

"Easier if you just…just let me do it. Won't t-take long." Herb had his tools laid out around him, and he lowered down to his stomach. "What's her name, by the way?"

Grady had been thinking about that since he was introduced to the ladies. The only woman he had ever had a crush on, except for Ms. Flowers of course, was when he was a kid. And it was Betty Boop. He had been convinced that they would be together, one day get married. He had fantasies of becoming a cartoon and the two of them living in a cartoon house in Toon Town.

"Betty. I think I'll call her Betty."

"G-good name." Herb got to it, tools clinking together as he worked.

Grady leaned against the wall and watched, and as he listened to the sound of Patty's light snoring just beside him, he started to doze off too. Even Lou, who had not left Patty's side since entering the restroom, had his had rested against Esmerelda's bowl, passed out. A steady stream of water spilled from the corner of his mouth and pooled beside him.

Grady had no idea what time it was, but he was sure that it had been the longest night of his entire life. Just imagining a mattress, a soft pillow under his head was almost orgasmic.

"Hey, Herb?"

The scrawny man turned his head, eyes huge and squinted, nose wrinkled, mouth open.

"Since you won't let me help you, would you mind if I went to sleep? I can barely keep my eyes open."

Herb smiled, wiped his hands off on his pants. "I'm all d-done anyway. Welcome Betty to the…to the family, ladies." He pressed Betty's flush handle, and she roared, sounded healthy, happy. The other toilets hissed in response.

Grady hopped to his feet, carefully pulled Patty from Esmerelda's bowl. The commotion woke Lou who smacked his mouth and scratched the side of his face. His fingers made a squeaky sound as they ran across the porcelain.

"P-Patty needs to sleep with her mama t-tonight, Grady. Good for both of them."

Patty wiggled in his arms, started to whine a bit. Grady quickly dashed across the bathroom, Lou right on his heels, and placed her into her mother's bowl. She quieted right away, sort of doggie paddled for a few seconds before letting her body float and falling back asleep.

"She'll be okay in there? All night?"

"Don't worry. Toilet babies can't d-drown. There's not a safer…safer place in the world for her."

Lou now had his head rested against Betty's bowl, and

was already asleep again.

"He's very protective. Always has been. He did the same…the same thing for all the other kids. Just let me know if h-he becomes a nuisance."

Grady yawned. "No, not at all. It makes me feel good knowing she's got a big brother to watch out for her. I used to wish I had an older sibling when I was growing up. Someone who could teach me things, someone I could look up to. All of my idols were fictional characters from movies."

The two men watched Lou and Patty sleep for a few minutes before Grady told Herb he was ready for bed. Herb showed him to his room, which was previously the kids' playroom. All of the bedrooms were lined up in the hallway that led to the restroom, spaced out like a hotel. Toys and books littered the floor, and Herb kicked a path for Grady. The bed was small, but more comfortable than the one he had at his old apartment.

"We'll get all this cleaned up t-tomorrow. Make sure you and Patty are comfortable."

"Thanks, Herb."

Even though he didn't really get a chance to meet the others, and he already had a run in with Gus, he felt at home. He had never felt so at home before.

In a matter of seconds, he was swirling off to dreamland.

 Chapter Six

John crept down the hallway, pressing his ear to the bedroom doors one at a time as he passed. Every one of them had snores coming from the other end, and when he reached his dad's room, he kept his ear to the door for an extra minute or so, just to make sure.

It's now or never, John.

His bag was already packed and ready to go, and his dad's truck keys were still in his pocket.

John had never driven a car before, but he'd seen it done on TV so many times, and the racing game he had for his Nintendo was the only game he could beat Lou at, so he figured he would be pretty good at it. Driving couldn't be all that hard in real life.

I'm really doing it. I'm free.

He pulled out the paper with Prettygirl18's address on it, kissed it, then wiped the water off before it made the ink bleed.

"Here I come," he whispered. *Please don't freak out when you see me.*

He gave the living room one last look, thought about all the happy times he'd had with his family, with Lou and Rosie. With his uncles. Even with his dad. The Christmas before last was especially great. Gus was in a good mood that day, surprised John with the Nintendo. He even got another box full of games.

His chest tingled and his stomach rolled as a potent panicky feeling swept through him. Water started to overflow from his mouth, but he sucked it up, wiped off his lips, and started for the door.

But it wasn't until he was across the living room that he noticed the light coasting in from the kitchen. Dim and yellow with dancing shadows casted onto the floor.

John's stomach churned, and he covered his midsection with both arms, doing his best to muffle the sound. But it was too late.

"John? What're you doin'?" Rosie was seated Indian style in front of the fridge. Her face was painted with brown smudges, empty food trays scattered on the floor in front of her. "Don't tell on me, okay? I was starving." She had the jug of urine-aid and gripped it with both hands, chugged some of it, then offered it to John.

John wanted to refuse, but was powerless against his hunger. He dashed toward her, took a long, deep drink, then replaced the jug in the fridge. Uncle Herb had prepackaged meals for them, and it looked like Rosie had gone through at least half of it. Even for her size, she had the biggest appetite of them all.

"You won't tell, right?"

"As long as you don't tell that I'm leaving," John said, then immediately regretted it. It was too late to eat his words because Rosie dropped the tray and stood.

"Leaving? Leaving where? Can I come? I wanna come too!"

"Shhh, be quiet. If our dads hear us, we won't go anywhere." *Shit, now what…?*

John took a seat on the kitchen floor, and Rosie sat back down to join him. John picked up one of the trays and popped it open, rolling his eyes as he took a long and penetrating sniff. He wanted to heat it up but didn't want the microwave noise.

"It's good cold too," Rosie said, then picked up the tray she had been working on, licked it clean. "So…are you really leaving?"

John moaned slightly as he chewed, rolling his tongue around and through the soft glory in his mouth. This was a good batch that his dad had brought home. It was always good, but this batch was especially delicious. Kind of chunky and spicy.

John spoke through a mouthful. "Yes. I'm leaving. And

you can't come with me because I'm not coming back."

"Not coming back?" Rosie tossed the tray along with the others piled up beside her, then scooted closer to John. "Why? You're my big brother, man. Right? How you gonna just leave me like that? And what about Lou? You're his best friend…me too. John…you, you can't go."

She clung to his arm then, leaned her head against him.

John had never seen her like this, and for a second, he wondered if she was right. Maybe his happiness wasn't as important as being with his family.

"I'm sorry, Rosie. I'll miss you. I'll miss everyone. But my dad's an asshole. I can't take it anymore, and I'm sick of staying in this house all the time. It's bullshit."

She clicked her tongue and shoved him. "Quit bein' such a bitch, man. You think your dad's an asshole? We all do. Be a man and stand up to him, puto."

"What?"

"You heard me. Me and my dad, we're sick of y'all yellin' all the damn time. One of these days, I'll cut that fat pig for real."

John realized that if it wasn't for him and his dad, the house would be peaceful. Sure, Ernesto and Rosie had big mouths, but besides that, they never caused any problems.

Maybe if I leave, Gus will leave too. He'll have no reason to stick around in a house that he clearly hates. I'm doing everyone a favor by running away.

"Well, once I leave, there won't be any more problems."

She stood, kicked the trays across the linoleum, making a crashing sound. John hissed, grabbed the tuft of hair on his head with both hands.

"You're such a pussy." And with that, she walked off, back toward her room.

John stayed seated on the floor, listening for the sound of his dad, or any of the dads, to wake up. Besides the opening and closing of Rosie's door, there was nothing He quickly cleaned up the mess on the floor, took a deep breath, and headed out the front.

As he made his way toward the pickup, he kept looking

over his shoulder, just in case. The coast seemed clear, but he still took it slow. He figured he could put the truck in neutral and push it down the road, get as far away from the house as he could before he actually started it up.

Just as he was about to get into the truck, he realized he never said goodbye to his mom. Uncle Herb had been in the bathroom installing Patty's mom, and by the time everyone had fallen asleep, John had forgotten about it, had been in too much of a hurry, too eager to escape.

He thought about going back, running into the house to say goodbye, to explain to her why he had to do this. But he knew he couldn't risk it.

Please understand, Mom. I love you. I'm sorry.

Tears flowed freely now, and he ran his arm across his eyes to wipe the blue streaks away.

He pushed the key into the ignition, threw it in Neutral, and started pushing. It wasn't as hard as he had expected. The house sat on a small incline, and once he got some momentum, John was able to hop into the truck and ride down the hill. When he was far enough away, he turned the key and brought the engine roaring to life, threw it in Drive, and took off.

Everything is going to work out just fine. Everything will be okay.

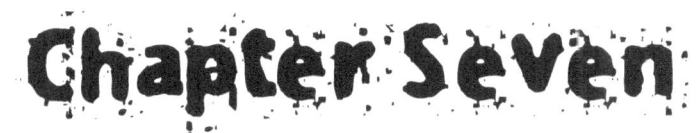

Chapter Seven

Grady woke up to raised, panicked voices. He was vaguely aware of Gus shouting and cussing before a door slammed and cut his rant off.

Grady had been engulfed in a dream, one of the best dreams he'd had in years. Betty Boop sat in a cartoon hot tub, but the hot tub was shaped like a toilet. Grady stepped in to join her, and even though the water was yellow and there were turds floating atop the bubbling surface like driftwood, it was nice. He waded toward her, and she handed him a glass of champagne. The glass had a face, and it smiled at him, urging him to drink its contents, and it wasn't until he sat beside the busty toon that he realized he was a cartoon himself.

"Is this real?" he had said.

Betty Boop didn't answer, just leaned over, puckered her lips. As she got closer and closer, her face began to shift and contort, and then it was a cartoon Ms. Flowers, and she reached behind her back, untied her bikini top, and…

"She's gone! I looked everywhere and she's gone!"

Grady sat up quick, threw the covers off. The voice belonged to Ernesto, and the kid sounded hysterical.

Who's gone? Patty?

Grady ran toward his door, stepping on sharp toys as he went, but he hobbled through, ignored the pain. The door slammed against the wall as he threw it open and sprinted toward the bathroom. The other men were in the living room, shouting and running around. Grady kicked in the double doors with a powerful hip thrust, and stumbled into the restroom, lost his footing and fell onto his stomach, knocking the wind out of him.

"Lou's gone…Lou's gone too!" Herb shouted from across the house.

Oh god…please. Please don't let this be happening.

The toilets sort of clicked, and Grady could tell by the energy in the room that this wasn't good. Something had happened. He army-crawled his way to Betty, trying to catch his breath the whole way. He lifted the seat and peered inside.

Empty.

He couldn't help but wonder if someone had come into the house while they slept, taken the children. Maybe someone followed Herb's car on the drive from Grady's apartment. Grady's body felt numb as he scrambled to his feet, imagining some sick bastard kidnapping his Patty. Shitting and pissing into the children's mouths.

"No…*no!*" Grady jumped to his feet and sped out into the living room. The house was a mess, furniture moved around, lamps and picture frames knocked onto the carpet. The rest of the guys were now out in the yard, every one of them shouting, and Grady raced out the front door and joined them. It was still the middle of the night, and Grady figured he hadn't slept but a few hours tops. "Patty's gone too! *What the hell is going on here?"*

"It's…it's the government. I knew they'd find us s-sooner or later!" Herb paced the yard, the veins on his face and neck standing out, his skin getting redder by the second. "They kidnapped them…p-probably doing experiments on them right n-now!"

"Fuuuuck!" Gus stood in the driveway, punching the air, his teeth bared as he growled. He stomped his way toward the other three men. "It wasn't no damn government. It was my boy. John did this. He stole my truck and took off."

Ernesto shook his head. "Rosie wouldn't just bounce on me like that. There ain't no way. You think John took them? You think he kidnap—"

"No," Herb said. "John wouldn't just take the kids like that. He's…he's more responsible than that, and John would never put…put his brother and sister in danger."

"Sisters," Grady said. "Patty's gone too, remember? My daughter…*my fucking newborn daughter!*" Grady's legs went wobbly on him, and before he knew it, he had crashed to the grass. Cold dew soaked into the seat of his sweatpants. He had never felt so helpless and terrified in his entire life.

"I'm tellin' y'all. John convinced the other kids it would be fun to go out. Probably told them it was a fieldtrip or some shit. He'd asked me to take him to the city before, said he's been bored here at the house. I never thought he'd do this…if I get my hands on that boy—"

"Th-that's the problem, Gus!" Herb said. "Maybe if you were a better father, hell even a better roommate, none of this would have happened. Now my Lou is out there…out there in the streets. Oh god…we have to go looking for them. We have to l-leave right now!"

"You don't have the right to talk to me like that. I never asked for this shit. I never asked to be a goddamn father."

"Neither did I, puto. None of us did. That don't mean you gotta be a dick. That don't mean you gotta beat on your own son." Ernesto looked Gus up and down, his lip curled.

"You motherfucker. You don't know the half of it. You don't—"

"I don't? I was seventeen when I had Rosie." Ernesto looked like he wanted to say more, but he just clicked his tongue and waved Gus off.

"What about the toilets?" Grady said, still sitting in the lawn.

"What?" Gus growled, peeling his hard eyes off of Ernesto to stare down at Grady.

"The toilets. Maybe they know something."

Gus smiled, shook his head. "You speak toiletnese, do you? Can't talk to a goddamn inanimate object, Einstein."

"But you can impregnate one? Have any of you ever tried talking to them?" Grady climbed to his feet, and before waiting for an answer, he was already jogging back into the home.

But he never made it to the bathroom. The TV caught his attention. The 24-hour news channel was on.

"Grady, Gus is right," Herb said as he burst in through the door. "They're not in-inanimate objects, but they can't talk. G-Grady?"

Grady barely heard a word. He had ears only for the news reporter with the hot pink neck tie. The elderly man had a smirk the whole time he spoke, his female co-anchor chuckling beside him. There was a graphic of a cartoon toilet with eyes and a smile beside the man's head.

"And the officer says he was attacked by some kind of creature. Said it looked like a cross between a child and a toilet. This is an actual report, folks, no joke here. The report came in literally a few minutes ago."

"Ohhhh, a were-toilet. Is there a full moon out tonight?"

As the anchors shared a laugh and began talking about the officer's mental health, Grady and Herb slowly turned to stare at each other.

"If that report just came in…they must be somewhere near the city, right? Maybe we can still catch them…" Grady still stared at the television, now showing a reporter standing outside the police station, saying that he just happened to be there when the officer came screaming inside, hysterical and shouting about monsters.

"We need to leave now," Herb said.

Grady was already running toward Herb's car.

Chapter Eight

Four hours ago…

Driving was harder than John thought it would be. And as soon as he left the forest that surrounded the house, he was instantly lost. He could see bright lights in the distance, and knew it was the city, so he pointed the truck toward it and pressed down on the gas.

But he couldn't keep the damn truck steady. The road was winding and curvy, and it seemed like every time he turned the wheel, he turned it too far, making the truck swerve. When he tried to hit the brake, he kept pushing too hard, jolting the truck, making the tires scream. He nearly hit another car coming the opposite direction. When they blared their horn at him, he flinched, lost control again and nearly spun out.

"Calm down, John. Take it slow." Water rushed from his mouth and soaked his jeans, and he gripped the steering wheel so hard, his white knuckles burned red.

The road straightened out some, and it started to get easier. Every time a car passed, John had a mini panic attack, but he was starting to get the hang of it. Before long, he passed a sign that told him he had officially crossed into the city limits. The buildings seemed to rise up out of the horizon as he got closer and closer, like concrete tree trunks with windows and lights.

He checked the rearview mirror every few seconds, trying to get over the panic that flooded his mind as he got further and further away from home. Even if he wanted to go back now, he had no idea where to turn. *I don't even know our phone number. No turning back now.*

The paper with Prettygirl18's address on it sat in his lap, and he kept running his fingertips over it, praying that she would accept him, that she would love him as much as he loved her. Of course, he never told her how he felt, but he knew he loved her. Just thinking about her made his chest hurt, made his palms sweaty and his mouth flood. He thought about the photo she had sent him, wondered why a gorgeous girl like that would need to go online to find a date. John had been chatting back and forth with her for a few months now, and he felt like he knew her, felt like he could trust her. He had come to her about all his problems at home, had stayed up all night venting about his dad, about never being allowed to leave the house. And she understood. She was there for him.

Of course, he never mentioned that he was half toilet.

John couldn't wait to see her. He figured they might need some time to adjust to each other, or rather, she would need time to accept who he was. To accept that he wasn't like other guys. But she would in time, John was sure of it.

His spirits began to rise a little, and he had never felt more alive than he did right then and there, cruising across the pavement, mere miles from what he assumed was downtown. He was finally free. He reached over and cut the radio on, turned up the volume and tapped the steering wheel to the beat.

When the flush exploded from behind him, he jumped so hard that he swung the steering wheel to the right, throwing the truck off the road and into the dry grass and gravel. John screamed as he tried gaining control, swerving left and right, spinning the pickup three hundred and sixty degrees until finally bringing the truck to a stop. His heart nearly beat right out of his chest, and water poured from his mouth as he panted.

The truck had a small back seat, just barely big enough for Lou to fit. He sat there, hugging his knees, his large eye quivering as it stared at John. The small pink eye leaked blue, blinked rapidly.

John was at a loss for words as he glared at his brother. He couldn't believe he hadn't seen him sitting back there, had been too caught up with his own thoughts to notice.

"Are you kidding me?" John signed. "What do you think you're doing?"

"I wanted to come with you."

"I already told you, Lou. You can't come. I'm taking you home right now. I can't believe you."

Lou shook his head. "No. If you're leaving, then I'm coming with you. You can't get rid of me." Tears stained his face. It sounded like something was knocking on his lid from the inside of his mouth.

"Lou, I'm not trying to get rid of you. That's not it at all. You're my brother. You're my best friend. How could you think that?"

Lou couldn't look John in the face anymore, and there was that sound again. Like a light knocking. Then Lou's mouth opened up and John gasped, splashed water all over the middle console.

He saw the fingertips first, tiny and sparkling white. They gripped the edge of Lou's lower lip. Then two twinkling eyes stared out, followed by a soft gurgling sound.

"Lou…what did you do?" John said this, too shocked to remember to sign. "This is bad…this is so bad. How could you be this stupid? Do you realize how screwed we are now? Oh god…oh my god…"

John leaned over and rested his forehead on the steering wheel. Water poured all over the floorboard and his feet, but he didn't care.

Patty giggled, climbed out of Lou's mouth and into John's lap. She reached up and grabbed hold of his lip, pulled on it, laughed as the water cascaded down onto her face.

Lou tapped John on the knee to get his attention. "I didn't want to leave her. We have to stick together."

"My whole plan is ruined. It's completely ruined." John sat up, pried his lip out of Patty's hands, then sat her in his lap and stared out the windshield toward the city. It was right there. He could practically spit and hit a building. But there they were, turned sideways in the grass. "We have to go home now. I have to take Patty back home to her dad. Jesus, Lou… she was just born yesterday, man." John remembered, then, that he didn't know how to get back home. *I'll try anyway. Maybe I'll be able to find it.*

Lou just blinked and rubbed his knees with his palms. He shrugged and John realized his brother wasn't understanding.

"We are going home. It's too dangerous for a baby out here," John signed.

Lou grinned, flushed his mouth. He reached out for Patty and the baby crawled across the slippery middle console and into his arms, cooed and gurgled, clapped her wet hands.

"You did this on purpose. You brought Patty because you knew—"

His words were cut off when the red and blue lights ignited out of the darkness and reflected off the truck's interior. The way the truck was positioned, the squad car had snuck up on the driver's side. John had been turned in his seat to face Lou and never saw it coming until it was right beside him, lights flashing.

"It's the cops," John said, not really sure what to do with himself. "I don't have a license, Lou. I'm not supposed to be driving!" Again, he spoke these words, or rather, he shouted them. Lou just stared past him, the lights dancing off his porcelain skin.

A car door slammed. Footsteps crunching over gravel and dead grass.

Lou quickly opened his mouth and placed Patty inside, ran a gentle hand over her head before closing his lid again. Her giggling was muffled but still audible.

Tap tap tap.

John felt like he could puke. He froze up, was too scared to turn and face the officer.

Tap tap tap.

These taps were harder, then another light exploded into the truck's interior, this one white and super bright. Lou shut his eyes and whimpered.

"Open up in there. Turn and face me and do it slowly." The officer's voice was male, but sort of high-pitched. "Do it now!"

"This is your fault," John signed toward Lou before slowly turning his head to face the officer.

The light came from a flashlight, and it was shining right

into John's eyes, but he was able to see the officer flinch and take a step back. "Take that mask off. Slowly!"

John put his hands up. "It's not a mask, sir. It's…it's just my face."

"You think I'm playing around here, son? Take it off."

John shook his head, couldn't stop the tears. He felt like he was about to crap his pants, but he knew if he did that, he'd burn a hole right through the seat. "I swear…I'm not lying. It's my face. I'm sorry…please, sir."

The officer clicked the flashlight off, and it was quickly replaced with a pistol. He aimed it at John through the window as he reached for the door handle with his free hand. The door creaked open, and John kept both hands in the air so the officer could see he wasn't trying anything funny.

The officer was a skinny man, his skin covered in orange freckles. His Adam's apple was big, looked like he swallowed a golf ball and it got stuck in his throat, and as the man stared John up and down, it sort of jumped and rolled around under his skin.

"See?" John said, hands still in the air. "It's not a mask." When John said the last word, a splash of water escaped his mouth and soaked the officer's shoes and the bottoms of his pants.

The man looked down at his wet feet, then back up at John with squinted eyes. "Get out of the car."

John did as the officer said. He wanted to turn and see how Lou was doing, but decided against it. It didn't seem like the officer had noticed him yet, or if he did he probably just thought it was a toilet in the back seat, and John wanted to keep it that way if possible.

"Put your hands on the truck and spread your legs."

John obeyed.

The officer patted him down, but only found the paper with Prettygirl18's address written on it. He studied it for a few seconds, then folded it, slid it into his pocket. Then the man grabbed John by the shoulders and spun him around to face him.

"Let me see your license and insurance." The officer had

lowered the pistol, but it was still in his hand. His eyes slid over every inch of John's face, and John could see him trying to figure out what he was looking at.

"I…I don't have one, sir. A license I mean. I'm sorry…I—"

"Can it, kid. No license, huh? What the hell you doin' out here? You're drivin' like a damn drunk."

John clenched his teeth, doing his best to keep from crying, but he couldn't help it. As the blue tears flowed, the officer's eyes widened and he took a couple of backwards steps.

"What's…what's the matter with your face? You got some kind of condition?"

"Condition? No, sir. This is just what I am."

"And what are you?"

"Well…I'm just a kid. A teenager. M-my dad works for the city c-cleaning sewers, and…and my mom's a…"

The officer had his head tilted and his nostrils flared as he waited for John to finish his sentence. His hand looked tight around the handle of the gun.

"My mom's a toilet. I'm…I'm half toilet and half human." It even sounded absurd to John as the words flew from his mouth.

There was a moment of silence, and for a second, John thought the officer understood. He thought that maybe the officer would help him, maybe let him go without getting him in any kind of trouble.

"Put your hands back on the truck. Now."

John hesitated, tried to find the right words to explain, to let the officer know he wasn't a threat, that he was really just a toilet kid lost in the night.

The officer grabbed John by the shoulder and shoved him, pushed him against the truck. "You think this is a joke, son? I don't take kindly to pranksters, you understand me?" He reached into the truck and pulled the keys out of the ignition, stuffed them into his pocket.

And then there was a flush.

"Holy Jesus!" The officer backed out of the truck so fast,

he tripped over his own feet and crashed to the dirt. The gun clattered away, but John didn't even look at it, kept his hands on the truck like the officer had told him to.

"Sir, I'm not lying to you. That's my brother in there. He's just like me...his mom's a toilet too."

Lou had climbed his way to the front seat, and he peered out, his good eye bouncing from John to the officer and back again. Then his lid cracked open and Patty stuck her face out, giggled and squirted water from her mouth. The thin stream hit the officer in the face, and he gasped, crawled toward his pistol, spat as he jumped back to his feet.

The officer held the gun with both hands, and this time as he pointed it, it shook. He kept licking his lips as he switched his aim from John to Lou. "W-what the hell is this? What's going on here?"

John wanted to turn and face the man, try to explain that they were just regular kids. That they weren't anything to be scared of. But there was no way he was taking his hands off the truck while the officer had a gun on him.

"What are you scared of?" Lou signed.

"D-don't move, goddamnit! The next time either one of you makes a move, I'll shoot. I...I swear."

"Sir," John said, his head turned, but his body straight. "My brother can't talk. He's using sign language, that's all. He wants to know why you're scared."

"Scared? I ain't scared. I just...I don't like being messed with." His voice had lost all signs of authority, and it reminded him of a child throwing a fit. The officer was taking careful, slow sideways steps toward his squad car.

It wasn't until the man was almost to the driver's door that John saw the figure standing on top of the roof, bathed in red and blue light.

Before John could yell a warning, Rosie dove onto the officer's back.

The gun went off three times before the officer dropped it, two of the bullets hitting the front of the truck and shattering the headlight, and the third hitting the front driver's side tire of the pickup and deflating it immediately.

"Get it off...get it off!"

John finally peeled his hands away from the truck and ran toward the struggling cop. Rosie had her butterfly knife clamped between her teeth, and she was smiling, hissing into the officer's ear. As he flailed around, water splashed from her mouth and soaked into his uniform.

Rosie pulled the knife from her mouth and pressed it to the officer's throat. "Nobody points a gun at my family, pinche pendejo."

He stopped moving right away, his lips trembling, eyes wide. The front of his tan pants darkened and John licked his lips as he watched the piss trickle out from his pant leg and run into the dirt. John was thirsty, and he could sure go for a drink...but he held back, tried to stay focused.

"Please," the officer said. "I have a wife...kids. Please don't k-kill me."

"Rosie, let him go," John said. "Sir, we aren't here to hurt anyone. My sister...she's just protective, that's all. She doesn't understand that you were just doing your job."

Rosie still had the knife pressed against the man's neck, and she shook her head and chuckled. "I understand. And protecting my family is *my* job."

"Rosie! Let him go...now!"

Something clung to John's shoulder then, climbed down his body like a cat.

Patty!

The baby was fast, and she crawled her way across the grass and gravel, latched her mouth onto the officer's pant leg, and sucked the urine from the fabric. The officer tried to kick her off, but Rosie pressed harder with the knife and he stopped.

"That's my new little sister, puto. If you hurt her, I swear to god I'll—"

"Rosie!"

She smacked her lips, rolled her eyes, and finally pulled the knife away, hopped off the man's shoulders. Patty drank happily, but Rosie pulled her away, held her protectively.

"I'm really sorry about this, sir. None of this was

supposed to happen…I swear. I didn't even know my brother and sisters were in the truck with me. I…I was going to meet a girl tonight. It's my first time out of the…"

But the officer wasn't hearing a word. It sounded like he couldn't catch his breath and he just stood there staring at them all. He looked like a kid in a haunted house, too petrified to move.

"You…y-you're monsters. All of you. G-goddamn monsters!"

Rosie flipped him the middle finger. "Damn right, bitch."

"No," John said. "No, we're not. You've got it all wrong. Please…"

Lou flushed his mouth. Patty giggled and reached for the man, wanting to get back to her snack. Rosie glared at the officer and snarled.

"Ahhhh!" The man spun on his heels and sprinted toward his squad car. The tires kicked up rocks and clouds of dust as they spun out, and then just like that, the officer was speeding down the road, toward the city, lights still spinning atop his car and splashing reds and blues all over the place.

"What a pussy," Rosie said as she shook her head. Then her scowl softened and she rubbed noses with Patty who gurgled and gripped Rosie's face with both hands.

John wanted to scream, wanted to pummel each and every one of his siblings into the ground. Break their porcelain, show them how mad he really was. But he collapsed into the dirt instead, clawed at the dry grass and gravel.

"So where we goin' now?" Rosie said.

Lou took a seat beside John, patted him on the shoulder. "Are you mad?" he signed.

John couldn't answer. He swung his attention toward Rosie who had Patty on her shoulders now. "Where were you hiding?"

"In the back. I wasn't about to let all of you guys have an adventure without me. Besides…you need me for protection."

"Protection? You're five years old!"

Rosie clicked her tongue. "So what? Got more balls than

both of you. And look at Patty. She was just born yesterday and she can already crawl."

John hadn't thought of that. "That doesn't matter! Do any of you realize what's going on here? That cop took the keys! And even if we had them, he shot one of the tires. We're stranded here. We're totally screwed, man. I can't believe this is happening."

Then John remembered Prettygirl18's address. The officer had pocketed that too.

"Shit!"

"Can't we just walk?" Rosie said. "The city's right there. Isn't that where you were goin'?"

"Maybe we should just walk home," Lou signed. "Our dads probably know we're gone by now."

"I...I don't know the way home." John stared down the road, doing his best to remember, but he had no idea where they were. He had just sped toward the city lights, took a bunch of turns without thinking about it, his mind on getting to his girl and nothing else. "We're lost."

Panic filled him to the brim, and he wanted his mom. He wanted to curl up into a ball next to her and let her comfort him. Hell, at that moment, he would even take his dad.

Something tugged on his pant leg, and he looked down into the big, blue eyes of Patty. Then the stench hit him, and he quickly covered his nose, staggered backwards.

"She's got a dirty diaper," John said. "Man, that stinks."

Patty kept tugging on his jeans, smiling up at him. Her porcelain lip was coated with drool, shone in the moonlight. John couldn't help but smile back at her, reach down and pick her up, despite the potent stench wafting from her backside. The diaper sagged, and he knew if she had another accident, it would start to seep out.

"Did you at least bring Patty more diapers? Clothes? Anything?" John signed to Lou. He could tell by Lou's face that he hadn't.

John didn't know what else to do but continue their journey on foot. He figured once he got there, he could find a computer, log on to the chat room, and get Prettygirl18's address again. Once he got to her, his love, she would help him. She would help them all.

***

The moon hung in the night sky like a urinal cake floating in black water. Grady concentrated on it as they sped down the road, all crammed into Herb's little Saturn. Grady had the seat behind Gus, which left little room for his knees. The car's radio said it was 5:58 a.m.

The men were silent. Grady had expected them to continue yelling, continue trading theories as to what could have happened, but he figured worry was starting to set in and nobody was in the mood to speak. Even Gus's anger seemed to have morphed into concern.

Then they spotted Gus's truck on the side of the road.

"Is that...?" Herb started.

"Stop the car! Stop!" Gus already had his door open before the car had pulled over.

Grady jumped out and sprinted, his stomach twisting into knots as he watched Gus fall to his knees just beside the driver's side door.

"What is it?" Grady shouted.

"Bullet holes," Ernesto said. He stepped forward and fingered one of them. "Those are fuckin' bullet holes, man. What...what does this mean?"

"What?" Herb shoved Ernesto out of the way and climbed into the truck, started tossing things around as if the kids would be hiding in the damn glove compartment.

"It means our kids are in trouble. It means they need us." Gus spoke under his breath, resting his forehead on the truck metal.

"They're not...not in the truck," Herb said.

"No shit, man." Ernesto paced back and forth, his eyes never leaving the bullet holes.

Grady climbed into the back of the pickup, not expecting to find the kids back there—hoping he wouldn't find them back there—but thought maybe there'd be some kind of

69

clue. There was nothing but empty beer cans and fast food wrappers.

"Now what?" Grady said. "Should we call the police?"

"And tell them what? That our goddamn toilet kids are missing? They'll throw us in the madhouse for sure. No…no we're on our own," Gus said, then slammed his fist into the truck and dented the door.

"No…Grady's right. The p-police." Herb squinted, the moonlight reflecting off his glasses and making his eyes look like big silver squares. "The guy on the news…he said an officer reported toilet monsters, right? We need…we need to find him. Maybe he knows something."

They all stared at Herb with hope in their eyes. Ernesto broke the silence.

"But what about the bullet holes? You think the cop shot at them? They're kids! Why would he do that?"

"Think about it. The guy pulls the truck over…and our kids are inside of it," Grady said. "They might just be kids to us, but to anyone else…"

"They're m-monsters," Herb said.

"Exactly. The man probably was scared out of his mind." Grady started toward the Saturn, waved his arm. "Either way, we need to get moving. We're not doing them a damn bit of good out here. Let's go!"

There was no more discussion as they all piled back into the car. Herb punched it and headed straight for the city.

Please be okay, Patty. Daddy is coming.

Chapter Nine

John's legs hurt by the time they had actually reached the city. It didn't look like it was as far as it actually was, but it had taken them at least a few hours to make the trip. It was still night time, and John didn't have a watch. He wished the sun would come up already, make everything seem a little less ominous.

"I'm hungry," Rosie said. "And tired. Can't we stop somewhere?"

The streets were nearly empty, a few hobos shuffling around. A brown Cadillac drove by, and as it passed, it slowed almost to a stop. The passenger window rolled down, and the driver and passenger stared at the kids with wide eyes, then shared a look with each other that said, "What the hell are those things?"

John hurried his pace, waved for his siblings to keep up. He suddenly felt like a freak, like a monster.

Our dads were right to keep us at home. We don't belong out here.

"Hello? We need some food." Rosie had stopped walking and had her arms crossed. "My stomach hurts, man."

Patty was asleep in Lou's mouth, but John knew once she woke up, she'd be hungry too. Lou signed, "I'm starving."

"Okay, okay. Where are we gonna find food out here?"

Lou jumped up and down, pointed toward the street.

Another car rolled by, and when the driver's eyes landed on the kids, the car screeched to a halt. The driver hung his head out the window, chewing something, smoke drifting from his nostrils. His mouth hung open mid-chew, the sloppy ball of food resting against his bottom teeth. "Wha…what are—"

Rosie bared her teeth and hissed, let water pour from her mouth.

The man screamed and peeled out as he drove off.

Rosie chuckled and shook her head. "Are all normal people little bitches?"

"Chill out, Rosie. Let's try and keep a low profile, okay? We don't want any trouble."

"We don't? Because wasn't this your idea to come to the city in the first place? What did you expect, for people to bow to you and give you flowers and shit?"

"My plan was to meet a girl. But you all ruined that! Now I'm stuck here with you, lost, hungry, and pissed off. So do me a favor and quit acting like an idiot, okay?"

Rosie looked physically wounded by the words, and she stuck out her flowery lip, turned her face away from John.

Lou shook John's shoulder, and when John turned to look at him, his brother was pointing at the street again. Lou stood on top of a manhole cover, and he pounded his feet on the metal disk, pointed at it with hard thrusts of his finger.

"The sewer," John said. "Lou, you're a genius. We can eat all we want down there. The same food my dad brings home."

Rosie still had her back to them, and John could tell she was trying to wipe her tears away before facing them. When she finally turned, she was smiling. "Hell yeah. Let's eat."

John knelt down, pried at the sewer lid with his fingertips, but couldn't get a hold of it. "Rosie, let me see your knife."

She handed it to him, and he slid the blade into the thin edge between the metal and the street, but he still couldn't open it. Couldn't even make it budge.

"Shit...it won't open. Y'all get down here and help."

Even with all three of them working at it, they got nowhere. John's stomach began to rumble, and he wanted nothing more than to dive into the sewer and gorge himself silly. The water in his mouth started to overflow, and he noticed the same was happening to his siblings.

John slammed his fist onto the manhole cover. "Come on...let's go. Get out of the open." John handed Rosie her knife back.

The three of them walked, sniffing the air. John closed

his eyes and let his nose lead him. He turned left, and the scent intensified, made his mouth overflow even more. His stomach roared, joined by the growls from Lou and Rosie's bellies.

"You smell that?" Rosie said.

"I smell food," Lou signed, then flushed his mouth.

They were in an alley between two brick buildings. Dumpsters lined the walls, stray cats and rats scurrying around, doing the same thing the kids were doing—searching for something to eat.

It started with a slight whimper. The whimper quickly became a scream. John had forgotten that Patty was asleep inside of Lou's mouth, and when he flushed, he must have woken her up. Her head popped up, shoving Lou's lid open with the top of her head.

She shrieked, splashing water all over the pavement. The cats and rats all sped away, terrified of what awful creature could possibly make a noise like that.

And that's when John noticed the other inhabitants of the alleyway. Their faces poked out of their hiding spots, their eyes stark white against the dirt and grime smeared across their cheeks and foreheads. They almost blended in perfectly with the night around them.

John wanted to get them out of there, was filled with the urge to run. He already had his hand on Lou's shirt and was pulling him backward, Patty screaming more and more.

These people didn't look scared. Didn't even look surprised. They had smirks on their faces, almost as if they had been expecting the kids to show up.

Rosie stepped deeper into the alley. "Any of you know where we can get some grub out here? We're starving."

"Rosie, let's just go. We can find somewhere else." John tried to grab her shoulder, but she shrugged him away.

"Why? There's food in here somewhere, I can smell it. And I'm hungry, man." She turned back toward the alley. "Come on. Hungry kids over here!"

A woman stepped out first, followed by a few others. The woman held a gray cat in her arms, stroked its back hard.

The cat struggled to get away from her, hissing and spitting and clawing, but she only pet it harder. The others stayed behind her, smiling like they had some secret they couldn't wait to tell.

"Who are you?" the woman said.

"You know what?" Rosie spat, hands on her hips. "I'm pretty fuckin' tired of you people lookin' at us all funny and shit. Chingao. We're toilet kids, lady. Get over it."

The lady only smiled, her teeth as black as her face. A soft giggle spilled from her fat lips. She nodded, dragged her feet as she walked toward Rosie, kept petting her cat. "I know what you are, baby. My question was…who are you?"

Before Rosie could say another word, John stepped forward. "What do you mean you know what we are? How?"

One of the dumpster lids flew open, and John flinched, grabbed hold of Rosie who already had her knife out. Patty screamed again, long wails that stung John's ears.

The figure that rose from the dumpster had white skin, his bottom lip smooth and shiny. He smiled wide and a sheet of water spilled from his mouth. "I know that cry anywhere," the man said.

***

Herb pulled the car into the police station parking lot, nearly crashing into a patrol car. The sun was just starting to come up now, and the station looked busy. A small group of officers gave him the stink eye, and Grady took the liberty of rolling his window down from the back seat.

"Sorry about that, officers." He gave a slight wave, but it wasn't returned. The men, all scowls and five o' clock shadows, went back to their conversation, sipping coffee and chewing donuts.

"Well let's get in there. Come on!" Gus said, his voice rough and deep.

"Maybe j-just one of us should…should go," Herb said, adjusting his glasses and turning in his seat to address everyone at once.

"What? There's no time for this shit." Gus swung his door open, had one leg out of the car already.

"Just…just wait a second. We can't just run in there like a group of cr-crazy people. I think…I think Grady should go in…alone."

"Shit, cool with me. I ain't in no hurry to talk to no pigs," Ernesto said, then shoved Grady in the shoulder. "Go, man. Let's get this over with."

Gus still didn't look happy about it, and Grady was still trying to figure out if he liked the idea too.

Herb placed his hand on Gus's shoulder, but the big man growled at him, and Herb quickly removed it. "You're upset. We all are. I'm just saying…if you go in there yelling at everyone…it w-won't help the situation. And Grady's got the kindest face."

"That's bullshit. I won't yell! I just wanna know where my son is!"

Grady hopped out of the car, wanting some fresh air if anything. He put both hands up and smiled. "I got this. Don't worry. I'll be right back."

Gus's face looked like an overcooked ham, but he slammed his door, slapped his massive paw onto the dashboard before crossing his arms.

Grady rushed past the group of officers, deciding it would be best to talk to a desk clerk. The station was packed, bustling with movement. It seemed like every single person was on the phone and shuffling through paperwork.

"Excuse me," Grady said as he stepped toward the woman sitting behind the front desk.

She held up a finger as she finished writing something down, her face loose and jowly like a bulldog. Her lipstick was a vulgar red color, some of it smeared onto her bottom teeth. Her nails were long and the same color as her lips, and when she finally looked up at Grady, she tapped the nails on the desk from pinky to thumb over and over.

"Hi…" Grady realized in that moment that he had no idea what to say to this woman.

"Sir, as much as I'd love to chitchat with you and get

to know you and all that, I'm gonna need you to get to the point." She smiled, but there was no joy behind it.

"Yeah...sorry. I saw a news story about an officer who said he saw—"

The woman held up one of her clawed hands, her red lips now a perfect arch. "I can't take no more of this today, you hear me? Ever since that story got out, we been gettin' all sorts of folks askin' questions. Newspapers mostly. Them funny papers that always be talkin' bout aliens and batboys. You with one of them papers?"

"No. I think...I think I might be able to help, though. If I could just speak with the officer."

"Help? Honey, he don't need no help from you. He'll be gettin' plenty of help. You a psychologist or something?"

"No, I'm just—"

"Is that all?" She had already taken her eyes off him and went back to scribbling on the paperwork in front of her.

"Please, this is an emergency. Those monsters he said he saw. The toilet monsters. I know who they are. My...my daughter's one of them, okay?"

The woman dropped her pen, stared up at Grady with eyes as hard as stone. "I really don't have the patience for this shit today, you hear me? I suggest you walk right outta here 'fore we charge you with making a false report. And wastin' my damn time."

Grady just pursed his lips and backed away. He didn't know what he expected this woman to say to him, but he felt even more helpless now than he did staring at the bullet holes in the pickup truck.

A few other officers had their eyes on him, some shaking their heads, others snickering.

These assholes aren't gonna help us. They think I'm crazy. Probably think their fellow officer is crazy too.

"Grady?"

The voice was vaguely familiar, a voice that had lived inside of his head for years. He turned and there she was, sitting in front of what looked like a detective's desk. It looked like she had been making some kind of report, but

76

she smiled up at Grady, stood up.

The detective sitting on the other side of the desk stood up with her, put on an obvious fake smile as he reached out and shook her hand gently. "You tell him to take all the time he needs, all right? And I know he's stubborn, but make sure he goes to the doctor, gets himself checked out, yeah?"

"I will. Thank you," Ms. Flowers said. The detective handed her some paperwork, and she took it, tucked it under her arm, then faced Grady again.

"What...what are you doing here?" Grady said. His hands ran up and down his thighs, and he quickly stuffed them into his pocket.

"I heard you talking to that woman," Ms. Flowers said. "She's a real bitch, always has been. The officer you heard about on the news...that's my brother. He's really messed up about all this."

Grady almost kissed her right then and there, and his shock must have been clearly written on his face, because Ms. Flowers grabbed him by the elbow and started walking. "Why don't we talk outside, okay?"

Ms. Flowers wore a white sundress that hugged her hips, and it clung to her tight frame once they were outside and a gust of wind hit her. Grady forced his eyes to the concrete by his feet, tried not to concentrate on her body for too long.

"What did you mean when you were talking to that woman?" she said, crossing her arms over her chest and chewing on her bottom lip.

"Look...I know it sounds crazy. Shit, it still sounds crazy to me. I'm new at this. Like...last night new."

"You realize that none of that made any sense, right?"

"I'm sorry." He took a deep breath, then pointed toward Herb's Saturn. Gus stood outside of the car, his forearms resting on the roof as he stared at Grady and Ms. Flowers. "I think maybe you better meet the others before I even try explaining."

Ms. Flowers used her hand as a visor as she squinted toward the car, then turned back to Grady with a wrinkled forehead. "What the hell is wrong with everybody all of a sudden? It's like I went to sleep and woke up in the Land of Oz."

"Let me just say that your brother isn't crazy. I know what he's saying sounds insane, but he's telling the truth."

"The toilet kids? He said they were like monsters. He can't stop talking about them. He's terrified of his own bathroom now."

"The youngest is mine. She was just born yesterday. The other kids...those are their fathers. They are real, and they are in trouble. They aren't monsters, they're just kids. And we have to find them and help them. Your brother is our only chance at saving our kids, and I can tell by how you're looking at me right now that you don't believe me, but...just come talk to the guys. You have to trust me."

She ran the fingertips on both hands through her hair and blew out a lungful of air. "My brother has been the most reliable, most stable person in my life since...well since forever. He's always been level-headed, if not a bit hot-headed. But a mental breakdown? No. Not him. Not out of nowhere like this. I want to believe him...I have to." She chuckled under her breath, reached and placed a hand on Grady's chest. "Let's go meet the guys. Tell me everything. My name's April by the way. You don't have to call me Ms. Flowers, okay?"

"What did they say? Who the hell is this?" Gus slammed his palm onto the car's roof with every other word.

"This is Ms...this is April. She's a teacher at the school I work at."

"How the hell does that help us, man?" Ernesto said, his window cracked just wide enough for his eyes.

"That officer from the news? That's her brother."

Gus and Ernesto both widened their eyes, hope spreading across their faces. Herb opened his car door and stepped out. The young orange sunlight reflected off his thick glasses, and April squinted as she looked at him.

Herb introduced himself, shook hands with her. When he spoke his voice was shaky, and Grady understood. The man was worried. Every second they weren't with their kids, it was hard not to imagine the worst. Grady did his best to hold himself together. Having April there definitely helped.

Herb had his wallet out, and pointed out all the kids in the family photo. April's mouth hung open, her head slightly shaking as she stared at the picture.

"Oh my god."

"Grady and P-Patty…they just joined us last night. Then this morning…all the k-kids were missing. And here we are." Herb pulled his glasses off and ran his sleeve across his eyes.

April had her eyes on Grady again, looked like she was ready to ask about a million questions, but Grady stopped her before she could start.

"We can talk more on the way to your brother's. You'll take us there, won't you?"

"Yes," she said without hesitation. "Meeting all of you will do him good, might help bring him back to earth a little bit. And I want to help you. I want to help all of you."

Gus clapped his hands once hard. "Good. Now let's get moving already."

"Grady can ride with me. You guys follow. He doesn't live far from here. But let me warn you guys now…he's a little on edge. If he points a gun at you, don't take it personally, okay?"

They all agreed.

As they sped down the road, Grady began before April had a chance to ask. He figured he might as well start at the beginning, explain to her how a toilet baby was conceived.

"Okay…so this is a little embarrassing to admit, but…"

Chapter Ten

The toilet man hopped out of the dumpster and splashed water all over the ground. It was dawn now, and dark yellow light poured into the alley like vitamin-rich piss.

The toilet man held something in his hand, and it wasn't until he got closer that John saw it was a used diaper, the middle of it smeared with a light brown paste. The man brought it to his mouth and ran his dark blue tongue across it.

John's mouth watered just watching him. His stomach erupted, and he had to control himself not to rush this guy and fight him for the snack.

"Where did you kids come from?" he said. He tossed the diaper to the ground. "I ain't never seen no other motherfuckas like me. Not never."

"What you gonna do to 'em, Head? You gonna cut 'em? I wanna help you if you gonna cut 'em." The woman with the cat snickered as she followed the toilet man down the alley toward the kids.

Rosie, still standing out front, walked toward the man, step for step, her butterfly knife flipping in her hand. "You get anywhere near my family, pendejo, and I'll cut your nuts off and flush 'em down your own mouth."

The toilet man, Head that woman had called him, ceased his walking, scratched the top of his head. Then he leaned back and cackled. "I like this one. Reminds me of me, you know what I'm sayin'?"

John didn't like where this was going, and he wanted nothing more than to grab Rosie, sling her over his shoulder, and make a run for it. But he couldn't make himself pull his stare away from that diaper, couldn't help but wonder how many more of those there might be in all the dumpsters lining this alley.

"Don't listen to this crazy bitch," Head said, then shoved the woman away from him. She slammed into the group of homeless people behind her, and as a group they all backed away from the toilet man.

They're scared of him. Maybe we should be too.

"I ain't gonna hurt y'all. Not my own kind, no way. Y'all hungry? That baby sounds hungry than a motherfucka."

Even though Patty screamed louder than ever, John had nearly forgotten about her the second he saw Head pop out of the dumpster like some kind of potty-in-a-box.

Lou shoved past John, Patty now scrambling to get out of his mouth. He started signing at Head, who stared at him like he'd been insulted.

"He in some kind of gang or some shit?" Head winced every time Patty shrieked.

"No," John said. "He's deaf. That's just sign language. He wants to know if you got anything we can feed the baby."

"What about us?" Rosie said, knife still clutched in her hand and pointed in Head's direction. "I'm starving, man."

"I bet I can scrounge somethin' up. But I gotta stay fed too, you know what I'm sayin'? Can't just be givin' all my grub away." He waved for them to follow him as he marched his way down the greasy alley. The soles of his rubber boots made ripping sounds with every step, as if the ground was coated in syrup.

As they followed, the horde of vagrants parted for them, but scowled, bared their black teeth, squinted their eyes. The woman with the cat made a hissing sound, petting the cat even harder now, stretching the skin around its eyeballs with every stroke.

"I was savin' this for later," Head said, coming to a stop next to a man who lay on his side, snoring like an old car engine. "But I'll let y'all have this one. Should be enough in there for the baby at least."

John could smell it, fluttered his eyelids as he inhaled deep.

Patty could smell it too. She hung from Lou's bottom lip, feet dangling. As soon as she dropped and her body hit the pavement, she was crawling toward the man's pants. The grime of the alley stained her knees and hands black.

The sleeping man, his clothes tattered and covered with filth, started coughing, his face a mess of wrinkles and boils. He turned his body, his front now facing the wall, his back facing the alley. His pants hung low off his ass, revealing a crack smeared with a dark green.

"Ol' Chuck here shit himself a couple hours ago. I was just lettin' it marinate, you know?"

And then Patty was on him. Her little white feet kicked as she dove into the back of Chuck's pants, sucking up the food in loud, wet gulps. Chuck kind of chuckled, nearly rolled over again with Patty right under him, but Head stuck a foot out and kept him propped up.

As Patty continued to feast, Head looked back up at John. "So talk to me, lil' man. Who are y'all? Where you come from?"

"I'm John. This is my brother Lou, my sister Rosie. Patty is our new sister, just born last night." John clenched his teeth as the hunger pangs became more violent. "Hey, mister…Head. Got anything else to eat around here?"

"What…you think this is charity? I gave you a freebie already, didn't I? I figure I already been nice, nicer than usual, you know what I'm sayin'?"

"Come on, Head. Let's cut 'em. You said I could. Last time you said I could, remember?" The woman reached for Rosie, plucked a hair from her head.

"Ow! You stupid bitch." Rosie swiped her knife, but it only found air. Then Head's shiny white hand was clamped around her wrist. Rosie squealed, dropped the knife.

"I lied," Head said, grinning. His teeth looked like broken porcelain, all jagged and sharp looking. Water trickled over his lips as he glared at John, but it was dirty, cloudy. "When I said I ain't never seen nobody else like me. I've seen plenty out here, lil' man. But this is my city, you feel me? Only room for one toilet 'round here."

"Let me help this time, Head," the woman said. "Let me help. You never let me help."

"Shut your stank ass mouth, Gretchen. I'm talkin' to my people right now."

Rosie slammed her free fist into Head's wrist, but it did nothing to loosen his grip. "Let me go, man. Let me go!"

Lou shook his head, clutched the back of John's shirt. John didn't know what to do, couldn't even will his legs to move. His entire body shook, and right then, he wished his dad was there. Wished his dad was there to stomp this bastard into the ground.

"Let her go. We didn't do anything. We're lost, okay? We don't even want to be in your city…we'll leave. We'll leave right now."

"Nah, lil' man. Y'all ain't goin' no damn where. You're mine now."

"Yeah," Gretchen said, and nodded at the group of vagrants behind her. She trotted toward Chuck who continued to giggle gruffly as Patty fed. Gretchen grabbed Patty by the ankles and lifted her. "Can I keep this one, Head? Can I?" She tossed the cat into the dumpster with a loud metallic thump and a high-pitched yowl.

Patty giggled as she hung upside down, her face covered in green muck. Her tongue slithered out and cleaned the mess off her face, and then she spotted John, Lou, and Rosie, reached out with both hands.

"Yeah, I don't give a shit. Keep the lil' motherfucka," Head said. He leaned forward, got nose to nose with Rosie. "I like this one. She's mine."

"Leave her alone," John said. His anger and hunger were beginning to overpower his fear, and he balled his hands into fists as he locked eyes with Head. "And tell that ugly bitch back there to let my sister go."

"Oh yeah?" Head said through a mouthful of rushing water. A wet laugh splashed out. "I bet you got big, shiny white balls, don't you, lil' man? You wanna see what I do to motherfuckas that think they got balls up in my city?"

Head backed up to one of the large green, greasy dumpsters, threw it open, stepped onto its ledge and jerked his head, motioning for John to take a look.

John signed for Lou to stay where he was, then slowly made his way across the alley. Head held Rosie by the back of the neck, smiling wide as his eyes ping-ponged from John's face into the dumpster.

John grabbed hold of the edge of the big metal bin, hauled himself up, and peered in. At first, he thought he was looking at discarded toilet seats. Which was disturbing, but something he knew wasn't all that uncommon in the normal world. But then he noticed the teeth lining the seats, the blue blood staining the white porcelain, a few dried up, purple tongues.

And a girl. A toilet girl. She looked about John's age, but had no clothes on, had her body curled into a ball to cover herself. She squinted as the sunlight hit her, her head shaking as she tried to lift it and peer out. Her lips parted, just slightly, and even that looked painful for her. An arm lifted, fingers outstretched.

Then Head slammed the lid, missed John's fingers by a centimeter. John stumbled backward, unable to find any words to express what he was feeling. He just knew he couldn't let this go on anymore, couldn't let the girl in the dumpster stay here with Head and his band of homeless minions.

And most of all, he couldn't let the bad toilet man hurt his family.

This asshole has to be stopped.

Head chuckled, held Rosie tight against his body. "Your sisters? They mine now. But you two," he pointed to John and Lou, "y'all's mouths are gonna look real nice in my collection."

Patty's giggles ceased suddenly from behind Head, and her eyes widened. Her face started to turn pink.

John grabbed Lou by the arm, pulled him forward. He signed to him quickly, then faced Head again who now had Rosie in a headlock. Rosie continued to struggle, tears running from her eyes in a steady blue stream.

"Hey...somethin's wrong with this thing," Gretchen said. "What's it—"

The yellow liquid sprayed from Patty's backside like water from a fire hose. It drenched Gretchen, coated her head, chest, and arms. She screamed, dropped Patty, collapsed to her knees as she tried to rub off the muck—it sizzled on top of her skin.

"It burns! Oh god...*it burns!*" She kicked her legs, and with each passing second, her scream grew louder, more piercing.

Patty gurgled as she crawled into the thick of the other transient men and women. The acidic fecal spray continued to erupt, coating legs and feet, burning flesh.

They all screamed now, falling to the ground and rolling around as they clutched at their wounds, only to have the stuff singe their palms, their fingers.

Head turned toward the commotion. "Goddamnit—"

John locked eyes with Rosie, and she gave a slight nod.

Lou stepped forward, inhaled deep through his nose, then unleashed a massive stream of water from his mouth. It hit Head in the face, blinded him for a second, but he still held onto Rosie.

"I said let me go, puto!" Rosie thrust her arm forward, then swung it back, her elbow connecting with a clinging sound.

Head let her go then. His eyes widened to the point that they looked like they might pop right out of their porcelain sockets. He stumbled backward, clutching his groin with both hands.

John rushed him, cocked his fist back, and slammed his knuckles into Head's mouth.

Head grunted, stumbled again, but stayed on his feet.

The transients writhed on the ground, and those who had escaped Patty's spray had climbed into one of the dumpsters and slammed the lid shut. Patty gurgled with delight, as if all her screaming victims were only playing a game with her.

John launched himself forward, but was met by Head's boot. The kick hit John in the sternum, collided with him so hard that he left his feet, crashed on to his back. His legs kicked as he tried to catch his breath, water overflowing from his mouth and puddling around his head and neck.

Head wiped the blue blood from his mouth, smiled at his painted palm. "You're dead. All of you."

The alley stank of cooking flesh, made John want to puke. He noticed that Gretchen had stopped screaming, lay in a heap of smoking meat and dirty clothes. Her face was gone, a grinning pink skull in its place.

The others now clutched shins and feet, the flesh melting off in sloppy pink globs, splashing to the ground. Spirals of smoke drifted off the exposed bone, adding to the potent stench thickening in the air. The screams were deafening, and John wondered why nobody was coming to see what all the ruckus was about. He had time to check over his shoulder once, saw a few people staring, but they quickly went on about their business, clearly not wanting to get caught up in whatever those crazy homeless people were doing.

John had just gotten to his knees when Head threw a punch. But just before it connected, Lou jumped in the way. Head's fist smashed into Lou's forehead, just above his bad eye.

Head yelped, pulled his hand away, held it to his chest and stomped his feet. *"Shiiiit!!*

Lou charged, the water splashing like rapids out of his wide-open mouth. He lowered his head like a ram, hit Head right under the chin. There was a cracking sound, and Head bellowed, clutched his face with both hands.

Lou's momentum had thrown him off his feet, and he lay on top of Head, pinning him down.

Lying beside the toilet man, covered in blue blood, was his lower lip. Cracks ran along the porcelain like spider webs, each one seeping blue. Head choked, tried to shove Lou off of him, but didn't have the strength. Lou's toilet water poured down onto Head's face, washing the blood away, only to be replaced by more as it pumped from his broken mouth.

"Get up."

John had finally caught his breath, and it was Rosie beside him, pulling him up by his arm. She glared at Head the whole time, then grinned wide, nodded toward the chaos going on at the back of the alley.

"Looks like our baby sister can take care of herself, eh?"

Patty was crawling toward them now, giggling the whole way. As she waddled past, the injured shrieked and shimmied to make way for her, each one of their grime-covered faces twisted with agony and terror.

John brushed himself off, then with the help of Rosie, lifted Lou off of Head. Lou turned, grinned wider than John had ever seen. The spot where Head had punched him had a small crack, and blood seeped out slow, ran down his porcelain in crooked blue lines.

"Did you see me?" Lou signed. "I kicked his ass."

"You did great," John signed.

Patty crawled over Head's face, and when her tiny hands sunk into the open wounds of his mouth, he shrieked as loud as ever, the scream sputtering off into a cry. His hands shook as they clutched his face, his fingers hooked and stained.

Patty smiled up at her siblings, reached her arms out to Lou. She cooed and smacked her mouth, wiggling her chubby, pale fingers. Then her face went pink again.

"No," Head said, his words sloppy, oozing out of his wounded mouth. *"Noooo!"*

One more spurt of yellow liquid sprayed from Patty's bottom, coated Head's face like caramel.

Lou quickly reached for her, scooped her up just in time before Head got to flailing his arms and kicking his legs. He wasn't screaming anymore, but sort of choking, making a sound like water draining in a tub. Blue smoke curled off his face as his body flopped, then his legs kicked two more times before he went completely still.

Lou held Patty out at arm's length, had her turned around, then spat a stream of water over her to clean off the acidic residue. Once she was sparkling again, he placed her back into his mouth.

Rosie spat into Head's face, then leaned over and picked up her knife. "Nobody owns me, joto. This is what happens when you fuck with our family."

"That's right," John said, mussing Rosie's hair and patting Lou on the back.

"What about the girl?" Lou signed. "Are we going to help her?"

"We have to," John signed. "We can't just leave her here."

John trudged toward the dumpster, climbed it, then slowly lifted the lid. The girl was in the same spot, now hiding her face between her knees, whimpering, refusing to make eye contact with John.

"Well hurry up and grab her," Rosie shouted from the end of the alley. "I'm starving!"

John held up his hand to her, then faced the girl again. "Are you okay? I'm not gonna hurt you. I'm here to help."

The girl moved her head just enough for an eye to peek out. Her brown pupil studied John's face, then she uncurled herself, but still covered her nude body with her arms.

John blushed, concentrated on staring at her face and the not the rest of her. He did notice that her ribs pressed up against her skin, and that she was covered with a black grime. Her skin had a light pink color, and she looked almost completely normal except for the porcelain lips. But they didn't stick out like John's. Her hair was brown and curly, just below her shoulders in length.

"H-he hurt me," she said. "The bad toilet man. He hurt me s-so bad." There was barely any water in her mouth, and what was in there looked gritty. Tears began streaming from her big, pretty eyes.

"He can't hurt you anymore," John said. "Me and my family...we're here to help you. Are you hungry?"

Her face lit up then, and she nodded, smiled.

"Hold on." John hopped from the dumpster and approached the moaning, crying horde of transients still writhing on the ground and clutching their wounded legs. One of the women wore multiple layers of clothing, and as John stepped toward her, she cowered, covered her face and head. "Give me one of your jackets and a pair of pants. Now, before I bring my sister back over here."

There was no hesitation, and the woman handed him the clothes, then crawled away on her stomach to put as much distance between herself and John as she could

John quickly raced back toward the dumpster, handed down the clothes. "Put these on, okay? Then I'll get you out of there and we can all go find some food."

With one arm still covering her chest, she reached up with the other and plucked the dirty, smelly clothing away from John. It would have to do for now. *Maybe Prettygirl18 will have something this girl can wear.*

John had turned his back to give the girl privacy as she dressed herself, then there was a light tap on his shoulder. The clothes were way too big for her, hung off of her slim body, nearly fell off completely. She smiled, though weakly.

"I'm ready now. What's your name?" Her voice was scratchy but mousy, sounded like every word must have caused pain.

"John." Then John introduced the girl to his brother and sisters. "What about you?"

She shrugged. "I don't have a name. I've never had a name before."

Once John had helped her out of the dumpster, she caught sight of Head's body, which still twitched every few seconds. Her eyes swung from his sizzling form to the others moaning toward the back of the alley.

"These are all bad people."

John almost put his arm around this girl's neck, just to comfort her, but decided against it. He didn't want her getting the wrong idea, and plus, he found himself a little flustered in her presence, felt his cheeks burning as he looked at her. When she smiled at him, he averted his gaze.

"Um…well maybe we should get going."

"Okay," she said.

"Wait. We gotta name her. We can't just call her Girl the whole time, right?" Rosie said. "What about Trashy since we found her in the garbage?"

"What? That's an awful name," John said. "Is there something you want to be called? It's up to you."

The baggy shirt nearly slipped off, but she caught it, pulled it over her shoulder and smiled. "I don't know."

Lou's mouth propped open and Patty poked her head out. She gurgled, looked like she was trying to talk. It came out as a bunch of slobbery gibberish, but toward the end of it, it sounded like she said Abby.

"Abby," the girl said. "I like that. My name is Abby."

"Abby." John nodded, smiled at his baby sister. *She's already starting to talk too? Is she some kind of super baby or something?* "Well, Abby. You ready to get something to eat now?"

Abby looked like she wanted to smile, but her face was pinched with pain. John wondered how long it had been since she had eaten anything.

"But where are we gonna go to eat?" Rosie said. "I ain't goin' down no more alleys. And we already tried the sewer."

Lou stepped forward. "I know where we can eat," he signed. "Just like me and my dad used to do when it was just the two of us. When I was a baby."

They all walked out of the alley together, John sharing a final glance with Abby before her already pink face grew pinker, then she turned away.

John's stomach growled, and he hoped Lou had a good plan.

***

April couldn't stop smiling as they drove toward her brother Dwayne's house.

"Like I said before...I know how crazy this all sounds."

She shook her head, and with her eyes still on the road, she reached over and patted Grady on the knee. "I don't think it sounds crazy at all. I think it sounds wonderful."

Grady visibly flinched. "You what?"

"Look. I won't lie. If my big brother wasn't screaming about toilet monsters...I might think you were crazy. But I highly doubt all of you got together and came up with this story just to mess with me. My brother is by the book, man.

So I have to believe all of this. And since I am now a believer in toilet babies...I think it's beautiful."

Grady wanted to be happy, but couldn't conjure the emotion as he again pictured his baby lost somewhere in the city. "We have to find them, April. I've only known Patty for a day...hell, less than that. But I love her so much. If anything happened to her, I don't think I could live with myself. In fact, I know I couldn't."

"I'm sure Dwayne knows something. It's all he's been able to talk about since last night. Just stay positive, okay? We'll find her. We'll find all of them. And once we do...I can't wait to meet them."

They finally pulled up to the house. April parked in the driveway next to the massive tan Ford pickup truck. The house itself looked clean, well kept. The lawn was lush and trimmed just perfect. An American flag hung from a pole mounted over the garage doors.

Herb pulled his Saturn up to the curb, left the engine idling as he and the others stared at April's car.

"You better let me talk to him first. I might be able to get him calm enough to talk to you guys," April said.

Grady nodded, was just about to exit the car when the gunshot rang out.

The bullet hit Herb's car just above the front passenger tire, but the engine sputtered and then died.

"Who the fuck're you and what're you doin' on my property!"

"Oh shit," April said as she threw her door open.

Grady tried to grab her but she was already out of the car and jogging toward the crazy red-headed man with the hand cannon.

Herb, Gus, and Ernesto were all ducked down as far as they could go in the car, Gus's head still visible because the guy was too big to hide in the tiny Saturn.

"Dwayne, stop it!"

Another shot, this one firing off into the sky because April had knocked her brother's arm away. She held his forearms with both hands, wrestling with him, but it didn't even seem like he knew she was there, had eyes only for the Saturn.

"They're friends, Dwayne. *Stop it!*"

"Are y'all with them? The goddamn monsters? Did you bring them here to finish me off? Because I'll tell you right now you got another thing comin'!"

He jerked his arm free, aimed the gun. The car rocked as the men did everything they could to protect themselves.

Grady couldn't make himself do anything but sit there and watch. He figured if he got out and ran toward this Dwayne guy, he'd catch a bullet no question.

Before Dwayne had the chance to get off another shot, April swung her hand and slapped him hard. The clap sound echoed off his face, but even that impact didn't seem to knock his sense back into place. He shook his head, blinked a few times, then aimed again.

This time, April cocked back a fist, drove it forward right into Dwayne's nose. Blood blossomed and his head rocked back. He stumbled a bit, a few steps backwards, then a few forward. His eyes finally landed on his sister, and he blinked as if just waking from a deep sleep.

"A-April?"

And then he fell, the side of his face slapping lawn.

Grady jumped out of the car, and by the time he was at April's side, the other guys were out of their car.

"Jesus, you knocked him out," Grady said. "Nice punch."

"I didn't mean to." April had rolled Dwayne onto his back, and she lightly slapped each cheek, but he was out cold. His orange mustache was soaked in blood.

"He deserves worse, that cocksucker. Could've killed us, man. That first bullet was inches from blowing a hole straight through me." Gus's chest and arm muscles looked tight, twitched as he glared down at the unconscious man.

"He's scared out of his mind. It's my fault. I should have called him first, let him know I was bringing company along."

"Toss his ass in the bathtub. Some cold water'll wake him up quick," Ernesto said.

"W-we need...we need to hurry." Herb grabbed a leg,

motioned for Ernesto to get the other. "Gus, you get…get the other side. Grab his arms."

Gus lifted the skinny man up with ease, could have probably carried him into the house by himself. They walked him toward the house.

At this point, some neighbors were standing in their lawns, and April waved to them, seemed to know them.

"Dwayne's just having a bad day. I'll take care of him, don't you worry."

That seemed to satisfy the nosy neighbors to a degree, but they still glared suspiciously, most of them elderly and wearing wide, dark glasses.

"Think they'll call the cops?"

"I think at least one of them probably already has. And since Dwayne is on leave for his mental health, we can expect company soon."

"I don't wanna be here when they get here. It'll just delay everything."

"I know. Let's do this fast. Then we can head out, find the kids."

"We?" Grady followed April into the house, which was spotless and had a calming Pine-Sol scent.

"Of course. I just knocked my brother out for you guys. You can't get rid of me now. I'm here to help, Grady."

Grady smiled in response.

The guys already had Dwayne in the bathtub, his legs hanging over the edge, bent at the knees. The back of his head rested on the soap holder.

"This asshole got any other weapons on him? Another gun strapped to his ankle, grenade shoved up his ass? Anything?" Gus had directed the question at April.

She rolled up both pant legs, but there was nothing there. "You check his ass if you want."

Gus just grunted, blew hot air from his widened nostrils.

"Y'all ready?" Ernesto said.

"Do it." Herb backed up a few steps, stood beside Grady and April.

Ernesto turned on the water, then switched it over from

bath to shower. The shower head hissed as it sprayed ice water over Dwayne's body, soaking him immediately. He stayed unconscious for a few seconds, then his eyes burst open, and he sat up quick, actually pointed his hand like it was a gun.

"Dwayne it's just—" April started.

Dwayne cut her off with a scream. It seemed like he noticed the men for the first time then, and he screamed again. Then his eyes landed on the toilet just beside Grady, and he pointed with a shaking finger, his terror seeming to get caught in his throat. He started coughing, kicking his legs to get as far away from the commode as he could. His body fell into the tub, the water raining down on him, splashing as he flailed. He finally found his voice and used it to shriek.

"Get it away from me! G-get it away!"

"Turn the water off already," Grady said.

Ernesto was snickering as he watched the officer freak out, then finally reached over and cut the water off. "Chingao."

April weaved her way through the men, motioned for everyone to back up. She knelt beside the tub, cupped Dwayne's face with both hands. His eyes were still on the toilet, his lips quivering.

"Dwayne, it's me. It's April. Calm down. We're here to help you, all right? There's nothing to be scared of."

"Th-the toilet...it wants to kill me. It wants to kill me so bad. I know it!" He wept now, hung his head and openly cried.

April hugged him, pressed his face against her shoulder. She looked at Grady, mouthed, "Get out."

Grady nodded, ushered the guys out into the hallway. Gus didn't want to leave, stayed rooted to the spot like a redwood tree.

"Gus, leave him be for a minute," Grady whispered. "Give April a chance to calm him down."

"This sonofabitch knows something. I'm gonna beat it out of him."

"No you're not. Come on. Try this method first, okay? If

94

it doesn't work, I'll help you beat it out of him."

Gus furrowed his brow, grunted, then turned and joined the others in the hallway. Grady lightly shut the door, then sighed, raised his eyebrows.

"I bet you my Rosie is the one who scared his ass so bad. Bet money," Ernesto said, looking proud. Then reality seemed to hit him and his smile faded.

Gus paced the hall, kept shooting glances at the bathroom door, swinging his fists through the air. "Goddamnit. This is such bullshit. My son...my boy...he..."

And then just like that, the big strong man collapsed to the carpet in tears. His shoulders jumped as the sobs hit him in waves. "I fucked up. I fucked up so bad." A string of drool hung from his lip and wiggled as he spoke.

"Gus...it's okay. John's a t-teenager. This kind of thing is...is normal," Herb said as he took a seat Indian style beside Gus.

"No, man. He left because I'm a bad father. I've...I've always been such a fucking awful father. Goddamnit. He deserves better...he deserves someone, anyone else but me." A fresh wave of sobs took him and he wailed and sniffled. "I didn't want kids. Never did. Always thought I'd make a lousy dad...and I was right. But I shouldn't have blamed him. I shouldn't have punished him for it. I'm a fucking scumbag, man."

"Look, man," Ernesto said, leaning his back against the wall just beside Gus. "I doubt any of us are angels, right? I mean, maybe that's why we got toilet babies in the first place."

"What do you mean?" Grady said. He didn't think he was a bad person, had never wished harm on any other human being. Except for himself of course. All those years contemplating suicide. And then actually going through with it, or trying to anyway. *Maybe Ernesto's right.*

"You never wondered about that? Like, why were we picked for all this? Me? I was all fucked up. Seventeen years old, slangin' dope, hooked on ecstasy. When I got real bad, I stayed in my room for a week straight, poppin' pills and

95

watchin' pornos, only came outside to use the toilet...sneak food and shit. Got so hooked on that shit, I couldn't tell what was real and what was in my head anymore."

Ernesto let his body slide down the wall until he was seated with Gus and Herb. Grady didn't want to be the only one standing, so he sat down too.

"I used my toilet...Guadalupe...a lot back then. Too much. Rosie had almost starved to death by the time I even realized she was born. Just floatin' there in the water, her mama hissing at me. I was scared...didn't know what else to do but go to my abuelita for help. It wasn't until I walked out into the living room that I smelled her. She'd been dead for days, just sittin' there in her couch, the Spanish novellas playin' on the TV."

"Holy shit," Grady said. He didn't mean to say it out loud, and quickly motioned for Ernesto to go on.

"I didn't know what else to do, man. I thought I was trippin', you know? After the cops came and they took my abuelita away... I figured I needed a plumber...maybe he could help me with my toilet problems. That's when I met Herb. He saved my life, man. For real."

Herb scooted closer to Ernesto and wrapped his arm around him. "I told y-you guys. We were meant to find each other. This is our family."

"Gwen," Gus said. He had stopped crying, had his forearms resting on his knees, his eyes bright red. "That's what you guys call her, right? John's mother?"

"That's r-right," Herb said. "John and me...we named her that."

"That's not his real mother. I don't even know if it's special like the other toilets, you know? I can't even fuckin' remember where I got it from."

"What?" Herb still had his arm around Ernesto's neck, his mouth hanging open.

"I'm sorry, man. I didn't know how to tell you...I didn't have the heart to tell John. His real mother...she was in a strip club. Ass Tappers it was called. I used to go there all the time...you know, before any of this. I didn't understand what was happening…didn't understand that the toilet was special…not until I met Herb."

Herb sat up straighter, adjusted his glasses. "It's…it's okay. We can still…can still go back and get her Right? Just show me where the place is…and I'll b-bring her home."

Gus looked about ready to cry again. He shook his head, covered his eyes with one hand. "It's gone. Demolished. After I met you and Lou, I knew I fucked up. I knew I had to go back and get her. Like I said, I just didn't know. I thought it was just a damn toilet. But when I went back, the whole place was gone."

Herb slumped over, stared blankly at the wall beside Gus. "She's dead. John's mother is dead, and it's all my fault."

"No," Grady said. "You can't think that way. You might have had some dark shit in your past…I did too. Suicidal, but I won't get into it. All this shit is crazy. This time just yesterday, I was living a normal life. If it wasn't for Herb… shit. Who knows what I would have done to Patty. I thought she was a dead rat when I first saw her at the bottom of my toilet bowl."

The men all shared a light chuckle then.

"Grady's right. W-we do the best we can. And you know…you know what? I think we're pretty damn good at it. Even you, Gus, you big ugly bastard." Herb playfully shoved Gus in the shoulder, and the big man laughed, ran his arm across his face again.

Then the bathroom door creaked open.

April stepped out first, sort of smirked when she saw all the men sitting on the floor like kids around a campfire.

Grady quickly wiped his tears away, took a deep breath to collect himself. "Well? How is he?"

Dwayne stepped out, rubbing his arm, eyes downcast. "I'm fine. Sorry I almost shot you."

The men all jumped to their feet simultaneously and faced the freckled cop. He held what looked like a crumbled sheet of paper, pinched between his thumb and the knuckle of his forefinger.

April snatched it out of his hand, handed it to Grady.

"That's an address. You guys recognize it?"

They all shook their heads.

"But that's John's handwritin', all right. Did he say anything?" Gus said.

"Said somethin' about headin' to the city to see his girlfriend. That's all I got before the little one jumped on my back and put a goddamn knife to my throat."

"See? I told you it was my Rosie," Ernesto said and slapped his thigh.

"Girlfriend? John doesn't have... Oh shit." Gus slammed a fist into the wall, knocking over a framed picture of Dwayne receiving some kind of award.

"What is it?" Grady said.

"The goddamn internet. I caught him chattin' it up late into the night a couple times, told me he had met a girl online. That's gotta be it. He's goin' out there to meet this girl."

"Well let's get moving," Grady said. "Because when this girl sees our kids...she might react like our friend Dwayne here."

Dwayne sort of chuckled, rubbed the back of his head. "I'd go with you guys...but I think I'd better stay here. I understand they are your kids...and believe me, it's a relief to hear because I thought I was going crazy. I just...I don't think I can see them. Not yet anyway."

"I'm coming," April said.

Dwayne handed his pistol to his sister. "Just in case. Oh..." He jogged into the kitchen, came back with a set of keys with a police badge replica keychain on it. "Take my truck. Sorry about your car," he said to Herb. "Bring my baby back in one piece."

"That's the plan," Grady said. "For all of us."

Chapter Eleven

"You sure about this?" John signed as they stood in front of the port-o-potty, staring up at the green plastic pillar.

"Me and my dad used to do this all the time when I was little," Lou signed. "Hand me that bucket."

The port-o-potty was sitting in the middle of a dirt clearing. Big yellow machines that reminded John of dinosaurs looked asleep all over the place. Huge piles of dirt and rocks were scattered around between the machines, along with big sections of scooped out earth. It didn't seem like anyone was around, so for the time being, it was safe. Patty sat in the dirt, the bucket on her head. She giggled and clapped her hands.

John pulled off the bucket, which had a long rope tied to its handle, and handed it to Lou.

"She's so cute," Abby said, then scooped Patty up and held her close.

"Be careful with her," Rosie said.

"She's being careful, calm down." John shot Abby a smile, then had to avert his eyes again once she smiled back. He turned and concentrated on Lou, who was now halfway inside of the port-o-potty's hole, his legs kicking.

"Is there really food down there?" Abby said.

"If Lou says there is, then there has to be," Rosie said. She seemed a little defensive toward Abby, but John decided not to say anything. He was too hungry to worry about it.

Lou backed out of the hole, held the rope in one hand. It looked heavy. When he turned to face the others, he reached up and flushed his mouth and smiled wide.

The smell was intoxicating. Every one of them had their eyes on the bucket now, even Patty, and as one, they rushed toward it.

Though he was nearly blinded by the voracious bubbling in his gut, John held back his sisters. Lou had already taken a big gulp of the brown goop.

"Let Abby go first."

Rosie pouted her lips, crossed her arms. John held Patty, had to use both hands as she fought to get to the bucket.

"You sure?" Abby said, taking the food from Lou and staring into his eyes with her big brown ones. Water poured from her mouth as she glared at the chunky soup. Flies began swarming around it.

"Sure," John said. "But you better hurry. We're all starving."

Abby wrapped her lips around the bucket and emptied the entire thing down her throat. The brown slop poured into her mouth, spilled some onto her cheeks. It was a mixture of browns and greens and grays, a few multicolored bits here and there. Abby ran her finger across her cheeks to get the overflow, licked them clean. She didn't seem to realize that she had just finished the bucket off. Then she started making choking sounds like a cat hocking up a hairball, and spat a wad of wet toilet paper into the dirt.

"I'm sorry, you guys. It's been…it's been a long time since I've eaten anything."

"Don't worry about it. I'm sure there's plenty more down there." John stared at the sloppy ball of toilet paper for a second before retrieving the bucket and handing it to Lou for a refill.

Lou climbed back in, scooped up another helping. John let Rosie go first before she killed someone, then let Patty get a couple of gulps before he finished it off. His eyes rolled as the thick stew rolled into his mouth. He let his tongue baste in the succulent paste before swallowing it down, the only thing missing was a big glass of Uncle Herb's urine-aide.

Lou went back for another bucketful, and they passed that around until everyone had had enough. They all patted their bellies, grinning satisfactorily. Patty lay on her back, blowing bubbles as she slept. Lou scooped her up and placed her into his mouth.

"God, I feel so much better. We goin' to your girlfriend's house now, John?" Rosie said, picking at her teeth with her thumb.

John noticed Abby's face turn a darker shade of pink, and she started twirling the dirt with her fingertips.

"Yeah. I still need to find a computer so I can send her a message."

Rosie stood, flipped her knife open. "I got this."

"Rosie, what are you...?"

But she was already jogging away. There were a good number of people walking both directions on the sidewalk on the other side of the fence they had crawled under to get to the port-o-potty. Important looking people, all fancy. Wearing suits, carrying briefcases. Most of them had their eyes on their phones, tapping the screens, sliding their fingers across it.

John couldn't hear what Rosie was saying, but he heard the woman's scream.

"Oh god. That's just what we need right now."

The woman dropped her phone and took off running in the other direction, both arms in the air. Then Rosie came jogging back, the phone in her hand, knife in the other, a huge toothy grin on her face.

"Will this work?" She tossed the phone into John's lap.

"Yeah...I think so." He wanted to tell her that what she did was bad, but he was glad to have the phone. He fired up the internet, and before long, he was logged on to the chat room. He immediately sent Prettygirl18 a message, then sat back and waited.

"Who's your girlfriend?" Abby said. She was now lying on her back, eyes squinted as she stared at the sun. "Is she a toilet? Like us?"

"Nope. John says she's a normal girl. He says he loves her." Rosie sat cross-legged beside Lou, leaned her head against him.

John just arched his eyebrows, not really sure what to add to that. He didn't know why, but he wasn't comfortable talking about Prettygirl18 to Abby. He wished Rosie had

101

kept her mouth shut.

"Is she pretty?"

"Well…I've never met her before. I'm hoping she can help us. I have to get all these guys back home before our dads go crazy. They're probably losing their minds right now." John ran his finger over the inside of the bucket, sucked off the brown sauce. "But not my dad. I bet he's glad I'm gone. That's why I'm not going back home."

There was an awkward silence then, and John found it hard to look at any of his siblings. He just wanted to get this over with, make sure they all got home safe so he could move on with his plan. He didn't know what to do with Abby, but assumed his uncles would help her, probably take her back to the house.

Briiing.

The phone vibrated along with the sound. Prettygirl18 had replied.

"It's her, you guys!"

Nobody seemed as enthused as he was. Then he realized Lou and Rosie were asleep, both leaning on each other as they snored lightly. Abby was awake, but sat with her back to John, holding her knees to her chest.

Prettygirl18: Where are you? I've been waiting.

John hesitated, not sure what to tell her about all that had happened.

BigBadJohn: Had a run in with the cops. Lost your address. Give it to me again and I'll be there soon.

She gave him the address, and he nearly responded by telling her that he had his brother and sisters with him, and some stray toilet girl they found in a dumpster, but left all that out.

BigBadJohn: See you soon. I can't wait to finally meet you.
Prettygirl18: Me too. I'll put on something sexy for you…

Even with the address, John didn't really know where to start. The phone looked pretty new, and he had seen on TV that phones had GPS now, along with all sorts of other cool things. There was an icon that said Map, and John tapped it. There was a blue dot that showed him his current position, and he typed in Prettygirl18's address.

We're only a few blocks away! Prettygirl18, here I come, baby!

John wondered if he could just leave the others there in the dirt and run to his girl's house alone. Then he could meet his girlfriend without any interference. But he couldn't make himself leave without them, so he stood, tapped Lou and Rosie on the shoulders until their eyes cracked open. Neither of them looked happy to be disturbed.

"I have the address. Let's go. We can call your dads from there, have them come pick you up."

"Can't you just call them from here?" Rosie said as she yawned. "You got a phone in your hand, man."

"I don't know the number..." John had been hoping that either Lou or Rosie knew it.

"Can't you just go to Uncle Herb's website? His phone number is on there. Then we can sleep here and wait for them to come get us."

It was a good idea, John knew. He didn't have the address for their current location, but figured he could probably use the GPS to get it. But that wasn't the point. His plan was to meet Prettygirl18, and he planned to do just that. After everything that had happened, there was no way he would give up on his mission now.

"You're right," John said. "I'll call them now, and they can come get you guys."

"Wait a minute," Rosie said, now standing and dusting herself off. "Where the hell are you going?"

"You know where I'm going."

"Not without us you're not." Rosie stretched. "We stick together. I'm coming with you. We all are, right Lou?"

Lou didn't protest at all, was already on his feet.

John smiled and nodded. Though they might embarrass him, he had to admit he felt safer with them around. "Okay. Let's go."

"I'm staying," Abby said.

"What?" John took a step toward her. "You can't. I mean...why? My uncles, they'll help you. You don't have to live out here anymore."

She just shook her head. "The city is all I know."

John knelt down beside her, and she turned her head so she wouldn't have to look at him. "Please. I can't leave you here. Come with us."

Now she did turn and face him, tears welling at the corners of her big eyes.

She's got the most beautiful eyes I've ever seen.

"Why? You said yourself you aren't even going home. So why do you care what happens to me?"

John wanted to drape his arm around her shoulders again, but decided not to. "I just want you to be safe, that's all. If you're with my family, I know you'll be okay."

"Then why are you running away if your family is so great?"

"Will you please just come with us? I want you to."

"Do you think I'm pretty? Pretty like your girlfriend?" She picked at a scab on her knee as she awaited his answer.

God, she is pretty. She's beautiful.

There was a tightness in John's chest as they stared into each other's eyes for a moment, a feeling he never had when looking at the photo of Prettygirl18. Suddenly, he found it hard to breathe.

"Yes. You are." Now John had to look away.

"But not prettier than your girlfriend, right?"

John snorted and smiled, playfully shoved her. She smiled back.

"Will you please just come with us? With me?"

A tiny hint of a smile crept onto her shiny, pink lips, then she stood, dusted herself off, and joined Lou and Rosie who stood by the port-o-potty.

"Okay," John said. "Let's get going."

Nobody responded, but they followed.

***

It only took about twenty minutes to reach the house. It was small, had an old beat up stationwagon in the driveway. The grass was overgrown, looked like a miniature jungle. Old newspapers were piled up at the foot of the driveway, some of them already turning yellow.

"Your girlfriend is kind of a slob," Rosie said.

"I don't like this," Lou signed.

"Come on, you guys. Can't you just give her a chance? We came all this way." John's hands spewed sweat and he couldn't control his mouth from overflowing. He took a deep breath. "You guys stay here. I'll go talk to her."

Lou grabbed John's shirt before he could walk away. Patty was awake now, was peeking out of Lou's mouth and gurgling happily.

"Please don't. I don't like this."

"Lou, everything is going to be fine. Trust me."

Lou's good eye quivered, and he pulled Patty from his mouth and hugged her.

"I won't be long. You guys stay out of sight until I meet her, explain everything to her. Then I'll call you guys over, okay?"

"Yeah whatever, man," Rosie said.

Abby just stared at John, which tightened up his chest again.

You can do this. This is why you came here.

John checked his clothes, brushed off some dirt from his jeans. He licked his hand, ran it over the patch of black hair and slicked it back. Then he walked to the front door.

There was a strange scent there, and the closer he got to the door, the more it intensified. It smelled like rot, like something had died. And he smelled food too.

His knuckles rapped a tune on the door, then he stepped back, stuffed his hands into his pockets. He thought he heard footsteps, but he couldn't be sure. Taking a few steps away from the door, he turned to check on the others. Lou's head was poking around the corner. John was about to shout at him to back up, that he didn't want to overwhelm Prettygirl18 with more than one toilet kid. Not yet.

Then he noticed Patty crawling on the ground. She was coming for him, but then turned and disappeared into the tall

105

grass. She giggled the whole way, squealed with delight.

John was just about to go for her, but the door opened up behind him.

Here it is. The moment of truth. Patty will just have to wait.

But before John could even turn around and face his love, strong hands gripped him from behind. A rag was pressed to his face, just under his nose. It smelled weird, strong. John tried to wiggle free, but he couldn't move his arms. Legs felt numb, wobbly.

And then everything went black.

Chapter Twelve

"Why keep them secret?" Herb replied.

"Well…yeah. I mean, I get you're scared for their safety and all, but I think people would react better than you think. Most people anyway," April said.

"Turn left here," the British woman from the GPS said.

There were only a few more blocks to go, and Grady's stomach started doing backflips. If anything happened to his little girl, his Patty, he didn't know if he could take it. Didn't know if he could keep the razor blade away from his wrists.

"I'd like…like to believe that," Herb said, staring at April's eyes through the rear-view mirror. "I just imagine the g-government sending over guys in spacesuits…like in ET. And they'll…they'll do experiments on them."

"I don't think that's true," April said.

"I don't know. People are fuckin' loco, man. I don't trust nobody," Ernesto said. "Except for my toilet brothers."

"Toilet brothers. I like that," Gus said. "And you know what? I agree with April. I think John deserves better than to be kept tucked away in a house his whole life. Besides, he's got his old man to watch out for him. If the government comes knockin', I'll shove my leg right up the president's ass."

"Turn right at the next stop sign."

"We're almost there, guys," Grady said, his voice quaking. He rocked in his seat, doing everything he could to stay calm. A hand was on his leg then, squeezed his thigh lightly. He looked over at April who smiled at him with pursed lips.

"You okay?"

"No. I won't be okay until I have my daughter back."

"Is that…it's Lou! That's my b-boy right there!" Herb

bounced in his seat and started slapping his window.

Grady saw the boy, and his spirits rose, but as they grew closer, he could tell something was wrong. Lou looked panicked, had water spilling out of his mouth in sheets. Rosie appeared then, had been crouched down in the tall grass.

"Rosie!" Ernesto rested his forehead on the seat in front of him, whispered something that sounded like a prayer.

As soon as the truck stopped, all of the men exploded out of it and rushed toward the kids.

Where's Patty? I don't see Patty...oh god...

Lou and Rosie both ran to their dads, both crying, both hysterical. There was someone with them, and when Grady had first seen the figure, he assumed it was John, but this figure had long brown hair, pink skin.

"Where's John?" Gus said. He stormed across the yard, checked along the side of the house. "Where's my son?"

Lou and Rosie were crying, couldn't get any words out.

"The bad man took him." The girl was sitting in the driveway, the back of her head resting against the garage door. She stared at all of them dreamily, her face blank. "The fat bad man in the house. He took him."

"What? Who are you?" Gus rushed toward her, and she curled into a ball as if expecting him to hit her.

"What about Patty? Where's my baby?" Grady was on his knees beside Lou and Rosie.

Lou started signing, sobbing the whole time.

"He says she crawled away and they can't find her," Herb said. "He says that...that John got pulled inside of the house, and Patty got lost in the grass somewhere."

Gus rushed toward the door and started pounding his massive fists on it. *"Open this fucking door right now before I kick it the fuck in!"*

Grady stepped into the grass, used both hands to part it as he searched. "Patty. Patty, where are you? It's your daddy. *Patty!*"

April joined Grady, checked the side of the house, grabbed the top of the fence, hauled herself up, peered into the backyard. "I don't see anything. The yard's small and I don't see anything but garbage back there."

"I said open up this goddamn door!" Every pound of Gus's fist was like a shotgun blast.

"We have to save him," Rosie said, both arms wrapped around her dad's leg. "We can't let that man hurt John. I'll cut him open, I swear."

"Who are you people and what are you doing on my property?" The voice came from the other side of the door, muffled and deep. "I already called the police. They'll be here any minute."

"Where's my son? I'm here for my son." Gus had his eye pressed to the peephole.

"I have no idea what you're talking about. Now get off my front porch and get the hell out of my yard."

"Open up this door or I swear to god I'll break it down!"
There was no answer.

Grady was now on his hands and knees as he circled the lawn, tall grass blades slapping him in the face.

"The gun," Gus said. "Where's the gun? I'll blow a hole right through that sonofabitch."

April held up both hands. "Whoa whoa. He said the cops were coming. I say let them come. We'll explain everything to them."

"No time for that shit, lady!" Gus punched and kicked the door, cursing and grunting.

The pink toilet girl was still curled into a ball in the driveway. She peeked out from under one arm and stared at everyone, rocking back and forth.

"There's gotta be a way in," Ernesto said. "There's always a way in, trust me."

"Everybody spread out. Check every window, every door. And keep a look out on the ground for Patty. She has to be here somewhere." Without waiting for a response, Grady ran toward the back fence, pulled himself up, and hopped over.

Then he heard the growl.

***

John woke up in a bathroom. The first thing he noticed was his headache. Pounding like a thunderstorm inside of his skull. The next thing he noticed was that he couldn't move his arms or legs. His head drooped, chin touching his chest. The light in the bathroom was so bright, and only made his headache worse.

What the hell is going on?

"Awake at last." The voice was male, not anyone that John recognized. "It's so good to finally meet you, Big Bad John. If I would've known your name was so literal, I would have begged you to come sooner. Just…just look at you."

John squinted at the figure standing in the doorway, but the light made it hard to see. Everything was blurry, and to open his eyes any wider than slits stabbed needles into his brain.

"Where am I? Who—"

It hit John all at once then. He had made it to Prettygirl18's house. Knocked on the door. He saw Patty crawling in the grass, and then someone grabbed him. *Did he just call me Big Bad John?*

"What's the matter? I'm not as pretty as you'd hoped?" The man started to laugh, but the chuckle was cut off by a phlegm-thick cough. "What's worse? Getting a man when you expected a girl, or getting a toilet when you were expecting a young boy?"

"Where is she?" John ignored the pain and opened his eyes as wide as they'd go. The blurriness began to fade and he got a good look at his captor. The man wore a white tank top, the part by his armpits and chest a dark yellow color. His skin was covered in black curly hair, and glistened with sweat beads under the bright light. When he smiled, he revealed teeth the color of cheese, blackening around the gums. A dark tongue slid across the top teeth, and then he started coughing again.

"Who are you? Where is Prettygirl18?"

"You still don't get it, do you, kid?" The man stepped

further into the bathroom, and it was then that John realized he was tied up in the tub. The back of his head slammed against the edge of the tub when he tried to avoid the man's touch. The man gripped John by the chin, squeezed hard. "You're looking at her." He puckered his lips and kissed the air, then started chuckling again.

John shook his head. "No. N-no. I saw a picture…you can't be—"

The man's hand darted forward and wrapped around John's mouth. It tasted salty and kind of sweet, made John's stomach turn. The man leaned forward, slid that dark tongue of his across the stubble on his upper lip. "What are you? Some kind of government experiment? No, wait. You're like some kind of radioactive mutant, right? Came crawling out of the sewer? Did you think you were gonna make a victim out of me, Big Bad John?"

John tried to talk, but the man's grip tightened. It felt like his porcelain lip was about to crack.

"I'm the one who makes victims, you hear me, toilet boy? As a matter of fact…I haven't taken my morning squat yet. And now that you're here…"

John's mouth was released then, and he took deep breaths, spat out the salty sweet taste of the man's palm. When he looked up, Prettygirl18 already had his pants down. His legs were covered in hair, thickest around his ass which he backed toward John's face.

"No! D-don't—"

Prettygirl18 spun and slammed his fist into the side of John's head. It hit hard, swung John's head to the right, cracking his face against the wall. He felt his lip crack as he yelped and moaned. Blue splashed into the tub, all over his chest and stomach.

Everything started to go blurry again.

And the next thing he knew, his mouth was being filled with fresh, hot food.

111

Chapter Thirteen

"Oh shit."

"What is it?" April said from the other side of the fence.

Grady stared at the Rottweiler as it lowered its head and took slow, tentative steps toward him. The growl grew deeper, more menacing. White, frothy saliva dripped from its mouth like beer foam.

Grady backed up until he collided with the fence behind him. He held up both hands, palms out. "Easy, boy. That's a good boy…don't come any closer."

But the dog didn't listen. It padded forward, licking its chops. Its black fur was matted and bald spots were scattered around its body. Its ribs pushed tight against its sides, deepening with every breath.

"Is that a dog?" April said. "I can hear it."

"Yes…it's a fucking dog." The words were no more than a whisper, and Grady didn't think April heard him.

"G-Grady…move aside." Herb's voice.

At the sound of the others, the dog grew more agitated. It charged Grady, but stopped just a couple of feet away, snapped its jaws in the air and flung spittle all over the side of the house.

"Guys…" Grady said.

"Move…move aside!"

"There's nowhere to goddamn move!"

The dog roared and lunged forward. Grady turned his head, squeezed his eyes shut, pressed his body flat against the house.

He waited for those frothy jaws to snap shut over an arm or leg, maybe tear something off.

But the fence exploded before the dog could get anywhere near him. At first, he thought someone must have used the gun, and though he was thankful for the thought, he couldn't help but think about how easily they could have shot him instead of the dog.

Grady's eyes burst open, just in time to see Lou flying forward, wooden shards needling through the air. Lou's heavy body landed on top of the dog, crushed it beneath his weight. The dog let out a loud yelp, but was still alive, still thrashing underneath Lou.

Grady expected the dog to turn its head and sink its teeth into the boy's face, but instead, it lapped at the water pouring from Lou's mouth. It whined softly as it drank, and Grady wondered how long it had been since the poor thing had any water, any food. Lou kicked his legs as the dog drank, as if it tickled him. Then the dog started licking Lou's face, making a squeaky noise as its tongue slid across the porcelain of Lou's cheek.

Herb and April stepped through the Lou-sized hole in the fence.

"I th-think it likes him," Herb said, then grabbed Lou under his armpits and hauled him up.

The dog jumped to its feet, studied the strangers for a minute, then sat on its haunches and panted. Lou stepped forward and scratched behind its ears, got its back leg kicking.

"Where's Gus and Ernesto?" Grady said.

Just then, they both came sprinting into the backyard through the broken fence, stopped quick when they saw the dog.

"It's okay. He's a good boy," Lou signed.

"Anything?" Grady said.

"Not a damn thing. All the windows have metal bars, and I couldn't pull the goddamn things off." Gus punched a new hole into the fence.

"Y'all check around back yet?" Ernesto said.

As a group, they all rounded the house toward the back.

***

The guy shit like it was the day after Thanksgiving. He filled John's mouth and throat quicker than John could swallow, and John had to breathe through his nose to keep from choking on it.

But Prettygirl18 was gone now, had waddled out of the bathroom, but kept the door open. John had managed to sit himself up, but no matter how hard he tried, he couldn't find the strength to wiggle out of his restraints.

He held onto the hope that his siblings would help him. He had thought he heard his dad at one point, screaming and yelling about something, but he knew that had to be a dream. Some kind of hallucination, probably from whatever Prettygirl18 had on that rag.

Something moved by the door. Something fast and white.

John furrowed his brow, sat up straighter. And stared right at Patty.

The baby smacked her mouth and gurgled at him, spilling a puddle of water onto the floor just inside of the bathroom.

"Patty," John whispered. "Patty, get out of here. Don't let him find you."

She tilted her head slightly, then squealed with laughter and crawled toward the bathtub.

"Patty, you have to—"

"And what do we have here?" Prettygirl18 stood in the doorway, resting both elbows on the doorframe. Tufts of hair shot out from his armpits like sea urchins. His eyes were locked onto Patty as she crawled her way up the tub and into John's lap. She hugged him, nuzzled him.

"You stay away from her!" John bared his teeth, pulled his arms with every ounce of strength he had, but couldn't get them loose. "If you touch her, I'll kill you. I swear I will!"

"John?"

The voice was so muffled, it was barely audible. It didn't seem like Prettygirl18 had even heard it as he licked his teeth and lips and ogled Patty, chuckling under his breath. Another phlegm-filled coughing fit took him, and as he hocked, John heard it again.

"John...is that you?"

Dad?

There was a small window just above the tub, vertical metal bars striping it from the outside.

"John, talk to me!"

That time, Prettygirl18 heard it loud and clear. But it only made him smile again. "Got a little family reunion going on out there. But I called the cops. Can't have people prowling around my house, now can I?"

"The cops will find me. And you'll go to prison, you asshole!"

"Will they?" The fat man stepped out of view for a second, and when he returned, he held a badge, breathed on it, wiped it on his shirt. "I doubt that, my pretty little commode."

Patty bounced on John's belly and giggled, paying no attention to the fat man across the room.

"Dad, I'm in here! Help! Patty's in here with me!"

"That useless fucking dog," Prettygirl18 said. "They say if you starve a dog, it makes it more ferocious, right? That retard in my backyard just got stupider."

"We're coming, John. Hang tight!"

The fat man shook his head and laughed, then stepped into the restroom.

His foot landed on the puddle of water that Patty had drooled onto the floor. Both of the man's feet flew into the air, and he crashed down on his back hard, smacked the back of his head on the linoleum floor.

"Boom!" Patty said, then clapped, crawled off of John and waddled her way toward the man.

Prettygirl18 moaned, coughed. It looked like he tried to sit up but couldn't manage it, his head crashing back down to the floor making a hollow thumping sound.

Patty climbed up onto his leg, up his torso until she was face to face with him. She hovered her face just above his and cackled like she was being tickled. Water poured from her little mouth, splashing over the man's face, filling his mouth and nostrils.

Something slammed against the back door. Then again and again.

Patty bounced on the man's stomach, making him choke and gasp as more water poured over his face, drowning him as the toilet baby chortled.

***

Lou fell backward, holding his head. The door was locked up tight, and was solid. Lou stood up to try again, but Herb caught him before he charged.

"N-no, Lou. You'll hurt...hurt yourself."

"What about this?" Rosie said, kicking a piece of plywood.

The wood was a small rectangle, and when she kicked it, it wiggled like it was loose.

"That looks like a doggie door," April said. "He covered it up."

Rosie tugged on it, but it wouldn't give. She pulled her knife out and started stabbing it, but she was only chipping away at it.

Gus roared forward, dropped to his knees, and started slamming his fists into the wood. The sound was sickening at first, and Grady winced every time the big man's knuckles collided, and after a few hard hits, the wood was smeared with blood.

"You motherfucker! Give me my son back!" Gus kept punching, now growling as he pummeled the wooden board. There was a crack. Wood splintered inward, and Gus kept punching until he'd smashed a hole right in the middle of it. He reached in, gripped it, and ripped chunks out, widening the entrance as much as he could.

Right away, the dog charged through it, disappeared into the house. Rosie tried to follow, but Ernesto held her back.

"I can fit! Let me in there, I can help him! John needs help...Patty's in trouble! *Let me go! Hijo de puta!*"

Rapid footsteps.

April pulled the gun out from her waistband and pointed it toward the noise, but it was only the pink toilet girl. She had such sad eyes, big and wet and brown, but as she jogged into the yard, they were wide with fear.

"Police," she said. "Right behind me."

Then the yard was swamped with officers, every one of them with weapons drawn. April dropped her gun before she was instructed to.

"Get on the ground! Now!"

"Our kids are in there! You have to help us!" Grady shouted, and stepped toward the officer.

But he was tackled from behind by an unseen officer, his face smashing into the yard and getting a mouthful of dirt. He turned his head and saw that every one of them was being held to the ground now, even April.

Then the officers noticed Lou and Rosie. And the pink girl. They exchanged looks, some of them lowering their weapons to gawk at the strange toilet creatures before them.

One of the officers took a long look at April, and he lowered his weapon too. "April? What the hell are you doing out here? What's going on?"

April had her hands over her head, and she moved them, squinted up. Recognition flooded her face, and she started to stand, but one of the other officers yelled at her to stay down.

"Relax," the officer said. "This is Dwayne's sister."

"And look. You see them? These are the toilet kids... the ones Dwayne was talking about. They scared him, but they're harmless...just kids."

The officer stared at Lou and scratched his head.

"Sir," Grady started. "My daughter is in this house. So is another kid. The man who lives here is holding them hostage in there...god only knows what he's doing to them."

The officer finally peeled his eyes away from Lou, who hugged Herb, hid his face in his father's stomach.

"A retired police captain lives here. You can't be serious—"

"I don't give a shit if the goddamn Pope lives here!"

117

Gus screamed from the ground, the three officers holding him down struggling to keep him there. "My son's in there, goddamnit!"

"Sir, settle down."

"Fuck you!"

Grady tried to stand, but was held in place. "Please. My daughter is inside right now. She's only a baby. Please help us…"

The officer paced back and forth a few times.

"Sir?" one of the other officers said, but was silenced by a raised hand.

The austere expression the officer in charge had been holding onto twisted into a grimace. He pointed at Lou, then Rosie. "What the hell am I looking at here?"

"He helped me. He saved my life," the pink girl said. "And I love him."

The officer turned to her, mouth hanging open.

And then the girl dashed toward the doggie door, dove through the broken wood and into the house.

***

John thought Patty had killed the guy.

Prettygirl18 didn't move much, just a few twitches of his leg. He choked every now and then, but that was it.

Patty still sat on his chest, but had turned to face John. She lifted one of her tiny hands and waved at him, then started gnawing on a finger.

"Good girl, Patty. Good—"

The man sat up suddenly, launching a wave of water from his throat that splashed all over the wall. He coughed, choked, eyes as red as rose pedals. With his cheese-colored teeth bared, he grabbed Patty with both hands, lifted her off his chest as he got to his feet. Then he turned her so she was facing him.

"You…little…you little shit."

There was a tiny fart noise, and then a spray of yellow erupted from Patty's backside. When it started, the man held her at arm's length, pointed her toward the wall where the liquid sprayed the towel rack and dripped down the wall, puddled over the floor.

The stuff sizzled as it began eating away at everything it touched.

"What the hell *are* you things?" Prettygirl18 said, then cocked his arm back like he was going to throw Patty against the wall. The veins on his face and neck bulged.

"Nooo! Don't!" John flopped around the tub as he fought his restraints, willed every muscle in his body to help break whatever was tied around his wrists.

There was a rapid click-clacking sound, then a growl and a series of barks.

A big black dog shot out of nowhere, latched onto the man's forearm. Prettygirl18 screamed, dropped Patty who landed on the dog's back. She laughed and laughed, riding the dog like a tiny bull as it shook its head and drew blood from the man's arm. Patty had fistfuls of the loose skin on the dog's back, and she soaked its fur as she chuckled.

"Ahhhh, you little bastard! Let go!"

With a strong jerk of his arm, he threw the dog off its feet, Patty along with him. The dog splashed into the puddle of yellow muck, immediately releasing the man's arm as it howled and whined, rolling around to try and relieve the pain but only managing to spread it all over itself.

Patty had been thrown off the dog, and she sailed across the bathroom right into John's lap, squealing like she was having the time of her life.

The dog kicked its legs, its fur burning away, the scent of cooking meat starting to fill the air.

"You little fuckers are dead meat, you hear me?" Prettygirl18 looked like he wanted to step into the bathroom, but Patty's mess had covered the floor. With a growl, he disappeared from view again, and when he came back, he held a black pistol that he pointed at the middle of John's face.

"Wait…you don't have to do this. Please…"

"You think toilets go to heaven, Big Bad John? Guess

119

you're about to find out." Prettygirl18 cocked back the hammer, grinned wide and orange.

There was a loud thunk. The gun dropped from the man's hand. His eyes seemed to cross, staring at the bridge of his own nose, and then he dropped to his knees, fell face-forward into the muck.

There was a sound like cooking bacon, and then Prettygirl18 was screaming, thrashing around in Patty's mess. Something had a hold of his ankles and was pulling him out of the bathroom.

Then Abby came into view, holding something hairy and rectangular in her hands. She stood over the man, a foot on either side of his chest. Prettygirl18 didn't seem to notice her standing over him like that, the object in her hands now held over her head.

That's the top of her head. That's her tank lid.

The man howled in pain, and his eyes popped open just in time to see Abby swinging the lid again, cracking it against the top of his head and silencing his screams.

Abby studied the man for a second before walking away from him and toward the bathroom. She still held the lid, long, curly brown hair hanging off of it, and she smiled at John as she replaced it back on her head.

The dog still cried out in pain, and John took a deep breath through his nose, and blew a wave of water from his mouth over the dog's smoking body. It washed some of the mess off, but John had to do it three more times before the dog was clean, and it lay on its side, whining, lets kicking. Most of its hair was gone, and spirals of smoke swirled off its bare skin.

"Hi," Abby said. "Your girlfriend is ugly."

John laughed. "Yeah. Yeah she is. Not quite what I had in mind." He winced as he sat up straighter, his wrists rubbed raw from whatever was holding them behind him. "But I guess I probably wasn't what he had in mind either."

Abby had both hands behind her back, sliding the toe of her shoe out in front of her like she was drawing an imaginary line. It was like she couldn't even look at John.

And just sitting there in the tub, unable to do anything but watch her, John couldn't help but notice how beautiful she was, how perfect.

"Hey, Abby?"

"Yes?" She still wouldn't look at him.

"I'm…uh, glad we met. Maybe…maybe me and you can…"

Doors crashed open followed by so many pounding footsteps, John was sure there was a parade in the house. The next thing he saw was Rosie. She looked out of breath, and when she saw John and Patty, and then Prettygirl18's unconscious body, she grinned wide, slapped Abby on the leg.

"Good job," she said. "You kicked his ass, man."

Abby giggled, finally looked John in the face. Her big eyes made his entire body tingle.

"Hey, big brother," Rosie said, then dashed across the bathroom, leaping over the remaining yellow gunk. She crawled into the tub, and using her knife, cut John free.

He sighed in relief, stared at his hands and flexed his fingers. Then hugged Rosie. Patty bounced and laughed the whole time, as if she never realized any of them were in trouble at any point during the day.

Then there were cops. Lots of cops, each of them with a gun drawn. When they found Prettygirl18 on the ground, some of them pointed their weapons at John while others moved deeper into the house.

"That's my son!"

"D-dad?" John wanted to be excited to see the man, but he found himself scared to face him. When his dad shoved his way past the officers and entered the bedroom, John started to cry right away, and he hid his face so Abby wouldn't see.

"Oh, John. I'm…I'm so sorry…" The big man ran across the tile, nearly slipping in the water and Patty's mess. His shoes sizzled, and once he was beside John, he kicked them off. The dog was under him now, still whining. "John, this is all my fault. I'm just so goddamn sorry, son."

When John saw the tears in his dad's eyes, tears he had

never seen except for when he was drunk, he didn't care if Abby saw him crying anymore. He reached up, wrapped both arms around his dad's neck, and squeezed. The two of them hugged for what felt like hours, and it felt so damn good. When they finally pulled away, Gus wore a huge smile.

"What do you think about coming to work with me, John?"

"What? Really?"

"Sure. It's perfect, don't you think? It'll get you out of the house. And hey, you won't even have to pack a lunch."

"That sounds great! But...what about your boss? He won't freak out?"

"I don't care, John. Not anymore."

They hugged again. John couldn't remember a time he felt happier.

***

Grady didn't have as easy a time as Gus when he tried to muscle his way through the horde of police swarming into the small house. April held his arm, and once the final officer had moved in, he followed behind, ignoring the man's orders to stay in the yard.

Herb followed orders, hugging his son, and when Lou tried to follow everyone into the house, Herb held him back. Ernesto was right behind Grady and April, calling out to Rosie who had rushed past the police, weaving her way through their legs, running ahead of them.

Once inside the house, the first thing Grady noticed was the smell. Like roadkill that had been rotting for months. The odor assaulted his senses, and he couldn't keep from gagging as they moved deeper into the house.

Then he saw the man lying on his back. Grady's heart began pumping faster. When he heard Gus crying, he immediately started running, shouldering his way past officers who were too busy to bother with him.

Please be okay...please be okay...

John lay in a bathtub, very much alive, hugging his

father. The dog, most of its hair gone, lay on its side, panting, tail slapping the floor.

And then his eyes landed on Patty. Rosie sat on the toilet, Patty in her lap. When Patty saw Grady, her face lit up, and she stared waving her arms and kicking her legs.

"Da!" she screamed. "Da!"

"Patty!"

The bathroom was so packed full of bodies that Grady didn't think he'd fit, but he didn't have to try. Patty had hopped out of Rosie's arms, and was crawling across the counter to get to her father. Once she was close enough, she dove for him.

Grady caught her, held her close, cupped the back of her head as he rained kisses on to her. She giggled and cooed, nuzzling him, spilling water all over his shirt.

"Is this…is this Patty?"

Grady turned to April who stared at Patty, mouth agape. And Patty waved to her.

"Didn't you say she was born yesterday?" April said. "And she's crawling, talking, and did she just wave at me?"

"She's special. Meant for great things," Grady said. "Come say hello."

April stepped forward, and Patty lunged for her, wrapped her little hands around the back of April's neck and gurgled happily.

"Whoa…hello there, Patty."

"I think she likes you."

Ernesto now sat on the toilet, Rosie in his lap. He was whispering something to her, and she was nodding and smiling. John and Gus both sat in the tub, laughing and talking. Just then, Herb and Lou stepped in, and when Lou saw Patty, he immediately flushed his mouth.

"L-looks like we got our family back," Herb said and patted Grady on the back. He reached over and tickled Patty under the chin.

"Sergeant!" One of the officers screamed from across the house. "Sir, you're gonna want to come look at this!"

The fat man, this retired police officer, started to moan

123

on the ground. Two officers stood above him, but it didn't make Grady feel any safer. He had to fight the urge to stomp the bastard's head in.

"Holy Jesus," another man said.

"Maybe we should get the kids out of here," Grady said to Herb.

Herb nodded, gathered everyone out of the bathroom. Lou had the dog in his arms, and they all went back outside.

And were greeted with cameras.

Epilogue

"Yes, Ma. I already told you."

"Well what's her name? She's not colored, is she? You know how I feel—"

"Okay...so yeah. Great talking to you. Goodbye now." Grady hung up the phone and smiled at April. "She's not ready to hear about Patty yet. Might not ever be."

April just smiled and shrugged.

Everyone sat in front of the TV, waiting for the news to start. John sat beside Abby on the floor, the two of them exchanging glances every few seconds, whispering to each other, giggling. Lou sat just beside them, his hand resting on the dog's head. As soon as they had gotten home, Lou gave the dog a bath. The burns weren't too bad, but there were bald spots all over the dog, who Lou had named Patchy.

Ernesto sat on the loveseat with Rosie beside him, Rosie unable to sit still as she waited for the program to start.

"God, it's taking forever. I'm gonna be famous now," Rosie said, beaming at everyone.

Grady had Patty in his lap. The baby had a bottle full of urine-aid, and she sucked it down while she kicked her tiny little feet.

April sat beside Grady, her hand locked with his. She smiled at him, rested her head on his shoulder. Dwayne sat on the other side of her, making googly faces at Patty and making her giggle.

Even from the living room, Grady thought he could hear the ladies hissing their approval from the restroom down the hall. They sounded happy, content.

"It's starting, it's starting. Everyone shut up!" Rosie was on her feet now, jumping up and down and pointing to the TV.

125

"Do you believe in monsters?" the news reporter said. He wore a fuchsia, pinstriped necktie.

"Monsters? That asshole," Gus said. He sipped his iced tea and shook his head.

"Officers were called to a suburban home today, home of retired police captain Blake Richards. A man that fellow officers say always went above and beyond during his time with the police force. They say he was a kind man, a good man. It was Mr. Richards who called police in the first place."

It switched to a field reporter holding a microphone up to an officer.

"I've known Captain Richards since I was a rookie. He taught me so much. I just… It's hard to believe."

The reporter's voice narrated as the TV started showing images from inside of the home.

"Once officers entered the house, they found that Blake Richards was living a secret life. The life of a monster."

"You're goddamn right he was the monster!" Gus ran his hand over John's hair and smiled. John smiled back, then made sure to fix his hair back the way it was. Abby leaned over and kissed his cheek, and John's skin turned pinker than hers.

The TV showed images of the man's bedroom, where at least ten computers were set up. Photographs of young boys and girls were pasted all over the walls.

"The former police captain was using fake screen names to lure young kids to his home. We're being told he operated under many screen names, each one a different persona. It was his screen name Prettygirl18 that finally got him caught."

There were close-ups of the photographs, and when it landed on a female, John sat up straighter and pointed.

"That's the picture he sent me!"

"What officers found in the other rooms is reminiscent of what you might see in a horror movie. The remains of over fifteen children, boys and girls, some of which have already been identified as missing kids that have been reported throughout the last few years. And who was responsible for

capturing this monster?"

"We are, bitch. The toilet kids!" Rosie pumped her arms like a victorious boxer, spun in a circle.

The others joined her, jumping to their feet and circling the living room like they were doing a rain dance.

"Some of our viewers may recall a report we did about an officer claiming to have been attacked by toilet monsters. Most of you, us included, laughed this off as some kind of mental breakdown. We had a chance to speak with Officer Dwayne Flowers just after the incident."

Then Dwayne's face was on the screen, a microphone hovering just in front of his mouth. Everybody glanced at him and his face burned bright red.

"I thought they were monsters. But I was wrong. These kids…they're special. And I for one am glad to know them. If there are any more of you out there…come forward. There's nothing to be afraid of."

The camera panned out then to reveal the kids.

"Yeah, not all of us are so special," John said.

"What do you mean?" Gus said.

"Well Abby…I'll explain later."

"We assure you that what you are seeing is real. There were no special effects of any kind used for this report. One of the kids, John, was held captive by Blake Richards, and it was him and his family that brought this monster to justice."

John's face on the screen now.

"I'm just glad he can't hurt anyone else. If it wasn't for my family, he might've hurt me too."

Now Rosie was on screen, scowling. She ripped the microphone away from the reporter and stared right into the camera. *"My name's Rosie. And I'm a toilet kid. That's right…we're real. But we're just regular kids, man. And we don't think we should have to hide from you people anymore."*

Then she spat water into the camera.

It cut back to the reporter sitting at his desk, his lips pursed, eyebrows arched on his forehead. *"And there you have it, folks. We've already had a few calls from others claiming to be or know of other toilet people, and all are saying that if it wasn't for the courage of these kids, they would have stayed in hiding forever. And now we…"*

The reporter continued on, but Grady had tuned himself out. He lifted Patty, blew into her belly and got her legs kicking. He handed her to April who hugged the toilet baby close, then leaned in and planted a wet kiss on Grady's lips.

"So," she said, twirling her finger through Patty's curl of hair. "If toilet babies are real…what else do you think is out there?"

"Who knows," Grady said, and stole another kiss. "Right now, I just wanna focus on my…"

A smell erupted into the air, and Grady and April both covered their mouths and noses. Patty sat between them, pink in the face, gnawing on her finger.

"Good th-thing she was wearing her diaper," Herb said.

Patty gurgled, pointed at her lap. "Poo poo."

They all laughed together. As a family.

SHANE MCKENZIE is the author of *Infinity House*, *All You Can Eat*, *Bleed on Me*, *Jacked*, *Addicted to the Dead*, *Muerte Con Carne*, *Escape from Shit Town* (co-authored with Sam W. Anderson and Erik Williams), *Fairy*, *The Bingo Hall*, and many more to come. He lives in Austin, TX with his wife and daughter. He's got plenty of pus for everyone, but it's first come first served. Don't be greedy.

"Pus Junkies" Shane McKenzie - Kip has the worst case of acne that anyone has ever seen. He has become an outcast in his school and the other kids call him Toad. But what they don't know is the pus leaking from Kip's acne is actually a powerful narcotic that produces strong psychedelic effects. Soon, everyone in school will want a taste of his hallucinogenic cream and this former-loser will become the most popular kid in school. But once you lick the Toad, there's no going back to normal drugs.

"All You Can Eat" Shane McKenzie - Deep in Texas there is a Chinese restaurant that harbors a secret. Its food is delicious and the secret ingredient ensures that once you have one bite you'll never be able to stop. But when the food runs out and the customers turn to cannibalism, the kitchen staff must take up arms against these obese people-eaters or else be next on the menu!

"Fat Off Sex and Violence" Shane McKenzie - Gary is a fucking loser. He spends his days jerking off to hentai and fantasizing about his ideal life. One day while sitting in his hidden spot in the woods, he encounters the perfect girl. She is his ultimate fantasy. The only problem - she isn't human. She's an otherworldly creature who feeds on acts of sex and violence. Lots and lots of violence...and she is a complete glutton for it.

"Muerte Con Carne" Shane McKenzie - Human flesh tacos, hardcore wrestling, and angry cannibal Mexicans, Welcome to the Border! Felix and Marta came to Mexico to film a documentary on illegal immigration. When Marta suddenly goes missing, Felix must find his lost love in the small border town. A dangerous place housing corrupt cops, borderline maniacs, and something much more worse than drug gangs, something to do with a strange Mexican food cart…

"Cripple Wolf" Jeff Burk - Welcome to Fetish Flights, the only airline where BDSM flight attendants service your every need. Aboard a red-eye flight from Tokyo, Japan to Portland, Oregon, a disabled Vietnam vet is harboring a secret. Every full moon he turns into a ravenous killing machine. When he transforms mid-flight and slaughters most of the passengers and crew, a Japanese punk band, a limbless superhero, a Muslim terrorist, and two stoner pilots must fight to stay alive until they reach land.

"Bigfoot Crank Stomp" Erik Williams - Bigfoot is real and he's addicted to meth! It should have been so easy. Get in, kill everyone, and take all the money and drugs. That was Russell and Mickey's plan. But the drug den they were raiding in the middle of the woods holds a dark secret chained up in the basement. A beast filled with rage and methamphetamine and tonight it will break loose. Nothing can stop Bigfoot's drug-fueled rampage and before the sun rises there is going to be a lot of dead cops and junkies.

"Night of the Assholes" Kevin L. Donihe - A plague of assholes is infecting the countryside. Normal everyday people are transforming into jerks, snobs, dicks, and douchebags. Today is the worst day of Barbara's life. The assholes are everywhere. But she must remain calm. If you raise your temper to an asshole you'll become one of them. After losing her brother to the asshole onslaught, Barbara flees for her life. She finds safety in a desolate farmhouse with six other survivors. Cut off from the world and surrounded by a sea of assholes, they must figure out a way to last through the night.

"Ass Goblins of Auschwitz" Cameron Pierce - In a land where black snow falls in the shape of swastikas, there exists a nightmarish prison camp known as Auschwitz. It is run by a fascist, flatulent race of aliens called the Ass Goblins, who travel in apple-shaped spaceships to abduct children from the neighboring world of Kidland. Prisoners 999 and 1001 are conjoined twin brothers forced to endure the sadistic tortures of these ass-shaped monsters. While the Ass Goblins become drunk on cider made from fermented children, the twins plot their escape.

AVAILABLE FROM AMAZON.COM

www.ingramcontent.com/pod-product-compliance
Lightning Source LLC
Chambersburg PA
CBHW020346260626
47156CB00004B/1691